Hamsadhwani

The Journey into the Melody of Carnatic Music

Bheema Shankar

Chennai • Bangalore

CLEVER FOX PUBLISHING
Chennai, India

Published by CLEVER FOX PUBLISHING 2024
Copyright © BHEEMA SHANKAR 2024

All Rights Reserved.
ISBN: 978-93-56489-60-8

This book has been published with all reasonable efforts taken to make the material error-free after the consent of the author. No part of this book shall be used, reproduced in any manner whatsoever without written permission from the author, except in the case of brief quotations embodied in critical articles and reviews.

The Author of this book is solely responsible and liable for its content including but not limited to the views, representations, descriptions, statements, information, opinions and references ["Content"]. The Content of this book shall not constitute or be construed or deemed to reflect the opinion or expression of the Publisher or Editor. Neither the Publisher nor Editor endorse or approve the Content of this book or guarantee the reliability, accuracy or completeness of the Content published herein and do not make any representations or warranties of any kind, express or implied, including but not limited to the implied warranties of merchantability, fitness for a particular purpose. The Publisher and Editor shall not be liable whatsoever for any errors, omissions, whether such errors or omissions result from negligence, accident, or any other cause or claims for loss or damages of any kind, including without limitation, indirect or consequential loss or damage arising out of use, inability to use, or about the reliability, accuracy or sufficiency of the information contained in this book.

Dedicated To

The lotus feet of my guru and mentor, "Padmabhushan," "Mahamahopadhyaya" Dr. Nookala Chinna Satyanarayana Garu, who is always a source of inspiration for me.

Praises

An informative and insightful look into the concepts and techniques regarding the stylings of Carnatic Indian music. Highly recommended reading for musicians of any level who are looking to enhance their knowledge of Indian music and culture.

– Billy Lease, music educator,
Guitar teacher, recording artist, and performer, USA.

It is sheer bliss and music as I read through the lovely book of Mr. Bheema Shankar. Undoubtedly a great journey into the melody of Carnatic music. Shankar gently takes us forward in this beautiful journey, not missing to introduce us to even the minutest of things. He showcases everything in a very picturesque manner. The narrative, so unique, brings every frame of the story, if I may call it so, as a scene in one's mind.

Shankar, a distinguished student of mine, three decades back, has many achievements and accolades to his credit. Really proud of him. I have the least doubt that each reader of the book will have the most satisfying journey. Wishing Shankar the Best. God Bless.

– Dr. A. Sabari Girish D.
Lit, HOD & Lecturer Vocal Music Dept.,
SV College of Music and Dance, TTD, Tirupati

Praises

Shri Bheema Shankar's book "Hamsadhwani" delves into the rich heritage of Indian classical music. He beautifully introduces the concept of Pranava Naada drawing insightful references from the Sama Veda and other ancient texts. The essence of Bharatiya Sangeetham fills the pages, deeply touching our hearts. Shankar's portrayal of musical saints is commendable. My heartfelt blessings to him and I look forward to his future with more literary works. With Best wishes.

– S. Dakshina Murthy Sarma,
Dean, National Sanskrit University, Tirupati

An initiative rather a storytelling par excellence, an eye opener so well-conceived and designed musically, not just for musicians but for music appreciation. I am indebted to learn many unrevealed facts.

– Debapriya Adhikary,
www.devasaman.com,
Hindustani Vocalist, Composer, Educator

The author takes you on an engrossing expedition as he unravels the roots of Carnatic music's vibrant melodies, rhythms, and traditions. The unique screenplay offers a refreshing read, effortlessly allowing you to soak in, savor, and embrace the essence of this timeless art form, without the hassle of tedious reading. Music enthusiasts, this is a treat for you!

– Sambavi Vigneswar,
Carnatic Music Vocalist, USA

The book with an enticing title, "Hamswadhwani: The Journey into the Melody of Carnatic Music," is an excellent script of music in text form. It touches upon the salient aspects of Carnatic music in depth and lateral dimensions and provides a thought-provoking narrative that bridges traditional and contemporary perspectives of music. His detailing and description of Pranavanaada, Saraswati veena, Gandharva Gaanam highlight his devotion to music, professional approach, and depth. In a chapter aptly titled "Dancing God", while dwelling upon dance-art forms in temple sculptures, his narrative is both heart-touching and emotionally evoking, scintillating. This book, with a total of Fifteen chapters, shall be very useful to beginners as well as professionals.

It is expected to serve as a reading delight and also a ready reckoner for various professional aspects of music. Having gained in-depth and adequate knowledge, Bheema Shankar has put his heart and soul into writing the book with such command and detail that this book can evolve interest to amateurs and established artists alike. My best wishes to all readers of the book to gain valuable insights. Blessings and best wishes.

"Vayuleena Vidya Deepika"

– Dr. Challa Prabhavathi,
M.A Music, M.A Telugu
Rtd Principal, S.V. College of Music and Dance, TTD, Tirupati

It is said that true musical knowledge (sangeeta and sastra gnana) can only be achieved with divine grace. I am delighted to share that both Mr. Bheema Shankar and I were disciples of Padmabhushan, Mahamahopadyaya Dr. Nookala China Satyanarayana Garu and adhere to his guru lineage (parampara). Renowned vocalist Bheema Shankar, aiming to make Carnatic music more accessible, has written an excellent book titled "Hamsadhwani: The Journey into the Melody of Carnatic Music." This book offers valuable knowledge not only for music experts but also for beginners. Without a doubt, I can affirm that Mr. Bheema Shankar's dedication and expertise in the field of music are truly commendable. My heartfelt congratulations to Mr. Shankar, and I extend my best wishes for the creation of more invaluable works in the future. May the blessings of the divine shower upon Mr. Shankar, ensuring perpetual success and recognition.

Apoorva Raga Gana Kokila, Sangeeta Sri, Sangeeta Saraswati

– Dr Potharaju Girija Seshamamba,
M.A., Ph.D., in Music,
L.L.B., L.L.M., M.A., (Hindi), R.B.P

Recipient of Limca Book of World Records,

Recipient of India Book of World Records

Founder Chairman of Sree Sesha Sai Sangeeta Academy

This book titled "Hamsadhwani: The Journey into the Melody of Carnatic Music," written by Sri Bheema Shankar Garu, delves into the intricacies of music, elucidating its impact on both plants and humans. It meticulously explores various aspects, such as Tyagaraja's compositions, the significance of sound, rhythm, and more. "Hamsadhwani" is a testament to Bheema Shankar musical insight and will undoubtedly enrich the understanding of music enthusiasts and students. I fervently hope that Bheema Shankar continues to provide such enlightening texts for future generations, imparting the divine essence of music.—Sangeetacharya Dr Vyzarsu Balasubrahmanyam

"Hamsadhwani" can be classified as a musical travelogue and a memoir. The author Bheema Shankar shares with us his fascination and quest for Carnatic music. Starting from Kanyakumari and ending the journey with Thiruvarur float festival makes me sit and enjoy the beauty and significance of these places. His quotes on the musical pillars of Hampi was an interesting anecdote. The way author Shankar blended the vedas, yoga, and the therapeutic value it brings gives a wholesome approach to the Carnatic music in the way it is being portrayed. I enjoyed reading

Praises

the nuances about every instrument. The approach has been very scientific and enough proof to substantiate the cause. The author's respect for Guru and other maestros shows his remarkable journey from a student to an inquisitive musician.

The reader's understanding of composers like Bhadrachalam Ramadasu, Annamaiya will go a notch up thanks to the wonderful incidents the author has given. The exemplary work of the musical trinities has been given a detailed explanation by demonstrating some of the popular works. The chapters on Gandarvas and Narada's musical genius highlights how rich and ancient Carnatic music is! It took me to my childhood memories as an avid musical listener and a student. This book would serve as a musical dictionary and guide for someone who is novice to the world of Carnatic music. It will also enthrall the ardent Carnatic musical lovers to reminiscent their experience and cherished moments. I wish author Bheema Shankar all the very best in his future endeavors. Thank you, With Best regards,

– **Srividya Venkat**
Indian Carnatic Violinist and Teacher
SV school of music, Rugby, United Kingdom

"Hamsadhwani" is a fascinating book of sacred Indian music with lucid language, beautiful anecdotes, fabulous paintings and engaging narratives that inspire and nourish the mind. Kudos to author Bheema Shankar for his marvelous effort to make spiritual, musical wisdom accessible to the young generation.

– **Dr. N. PADMA**
Professor (Retd) & H. O. D (Former),
Dept. of Performing Arts,
Sri Venkateswara University,
Tirupati

Index

Praises..iv
Index..ix
Introduction..x

Chapter 1. The Beginning..1
Chapter 2. Singing Stones 14
Chapter 3. Pranava Naada– Om 21
Chapter 4. Vrindavan Mellows..................................35
Chapter 5. Tiruvarur Connection..............................45
Chapter 6. Dancing God 66
Chapter 7. Sabha..81
Chapter 8. Saraswati Veena 94
Chapter 9. Gandharva Gaanam 101
Chapter 10. Fidelu 116
Chapter 11. Beats And Heart Beats 124
Chapter 12. Haridasu 131
Chapter 13. Madhuram..145
Chapter 14. The Float Festival 154

Echoes Of Ragas: Exploring Listener's Choice.....166
References 214
Glossary 216
Acknowledgments...221
Praises For The Book 224
About The Author...228

Introduction

The book in your hands is written with the aspiration of exploring the rich tapestry of South Indian Classical Music (Carnatic Music), offering insights into its profound significance and timeless traditions. I hope you have a magnificent journey as we proceed together through the pages of this book.

Chapter 1, titled "The Beginning," sets the stage by elucidating the profound benefits of immersing oneself in the world of Classical music, with a specific focus on the enchanting realm of Indian Classical Music.

Chapter 2, "Singing Stones," takes us to the majestic pillars of Hampi, where the seven notes of Indian Classical Music, known as the "Saptaswara," stand as musical pillars, guiding us through the intricacies of this ancient art form.

"PranavaNaada-OM," Chapter 3, unveils the significance of the sacred syllable OM and traces its roots to the origin of Carnatic music, offering a deeper understanding of the spiritual dimensions intertwined with the melody.

Venturing into the world of instruments, Chapter 4, "Vrindavan Mellows," introduces the flute and shares delightful anecdotes, weaving a melodic tapestry around this enchanting musical companion.

"Tiruvarur Connection," in Chapter 5, takes us on a journey to the Tyagaraja Swamy temple, offering a glimpse into the sanctum of inspiration and stories of saints who shaped the trinity of music.

Dive into the rhythm of Chapter 6, "Dancing God," as we explore the celestial dance of Nataraja at Ajapa Mandapam in Tiruvarur, that resonates with the essence of Carnatic music.

"Sabha," Chapter 7, traces the evolution of concerts, providing a guide on how to truly listen and appreciate the intricate layers of musical expression, offering a backstage pass to the musician's experience.

Chapters 8 through Chapter 11, unravel the tales behind the musical instruments, featuring the veena, vocal singing, violin, and percussion, showcasing the diverse palette of sounds that form the backbone of Carnatic music.

In Chapter 12, "Haridasu," we explore the soulful singing of Haridas and delve into the storytelling art form of "Harikatha," offering glimpses into the lives of musical luminaries like Purandaradasa and Bhadrachala Ramadasu.

Chapter 13 – Madhuram – In this chapter, you'll read about different composers like Annamacharya, Narayana Theertha, Jayadeva, and Kshetrayya. It introduces their "madhura bhakti," which is their sweet devotion and love for God.

Chapter 14 – "The Float Festival," unfolds as the magnificent finale, inviting us to a concert set amidst the enchanting ambiance of Tiruvarur Tyagaraja Swamy temple during the float festival.

The Chapter describes a concert at the float festival (Theppam) at Tiruvarur Tyagaraja Swamy temple.

Echoes of Ragas: Exploring Listener's Choice – In this section, you'll get to know some popular Ragas in Carnatic music. It suggests songs and artists you can listen to, and how to find them online.

CHAPTER 1

THE BEGINNING

$\mathcal{B}$oarding a ferry from the shores of Kanyakumari, I embarked on a serene journey towards the iconic Vivekananda Rock Memorial. The gentle waves cradled the boat, and the anticipation of the experience ahead heightened as we approached the sacred rock.

Visiting Vivekananda Rock in Kanyakumari, Tamil Nadu, India, I experienced a captivating moment as the Bay of Bengal, Indian Ocean, and Arabian Sea came together at this meeting point. The sounds of the waves blended with the peaceful aura of the rock, creating an atmosphere steeped in spirituality with great history.

Kanyakumari is at the very southern tip of India. It holds the distinction of being the southernmost city on mainland India, earning the epithet "The Land's End." The iconic Vivekananda rock was built in honor of Swami Vivekananda. It is said that Vivekananda had attained enlightenment on the rock.

The salty breeze danced through the seashore as I sat on the mid-sea rock overlooking the vast expanse of the ocean. The talam of waves crashing against the shore echoed in my ears like the sound of mridangam, a soothing melody with perfect sruthi that seemed to have gone through my mind, meditating on Swami Vivekananda.

Swami Vivekananda is said to have crossed the seashore in Kanyakumari, swimming to the mid-sea rock, where he meditated for three days and nights, ultimately achieving enlightenment. He was a disciple of Sri Ramakrishna, the 19th-century Indian mystic, yogi, spiritual teacher, social reformer, and profound scholar. Swami Vivekananda's books are very influential. Swami spread the philosophies of Yoga and Vedanta from India to Western countries. The great poet Rabindranath Tagore says – "*If you want to know India, study Vivekananda.*"

Vivekananda: A Gifted Musician

Swami Vivekananda was blessed with a sweet voice and a high degree of proficiency in music. Not many people know that Swami Vivekananda was a knowledgeable musician. Vivekananda started learning music from his father and later got vocal training, focusing on the Dhrupad style of Indian classical music. He used to sing for several hours and enthralled the listeners. Vivekananda was a talented singer and musician. He played the flute, sitar, and sarangi flawlessly. He also wrote and sang most of the bhajans and songs about Paramhans.

In one of his lectures in California, he mentioned that music and dance are considered to be religions in India. He stated that if one puts their soul into a song, they attain salvation. He said that music is the highest art and to those who understand that, it's the highest form of worship.

Effect of Music on the Mind

Vivekananda declares that music has a tremendous effect on the human mind.

Chandogya Upanishad says that our minds are super important and even more potent than our speech. Our minds are the bosses of our lives because without them working well, we wouldn't be able to talk, name things, or learn new stuff.

Everything we do, we do with our minds. When we talk about ourselves, we're talking about our minds. It's like saying, "It's me!"—that "me" is our mind.

Minds do amazing things. Since 2006, two professors at the University of Central Florida have been teaching a highly popular course in The Burnett Honors College titled "Music and the Brain". They've found that music can do wonders, like making us feel less stressed and easing pain. It even improves our brains by enhancing our thinking and movement.

Birds Learn Songs

Scientists at the University of Central Florida conducted neurological studies on songbirds like canaries.

They discovered that these birds stop singing during the fall because the brain cells that help them sing, die. But don't worry! During the winter, those brain cells grow back, and in the spring, the birds learn their songs all over again. This makes the scientists think that listening to music might also help our brains grow new cells!

Comfort for Wounded Soldiers

Research shows that music brings relief to soldiers injured in war, helping ease anxiety and support the healing of their brains. Music acts like medicine for the mind. Soldiers facing tough times with injuries become withdrawn, but music becomes their new way of communicating. Music researchers emphasize the power of music, equating it with spoken words, and underscoring how it can transform and bring life to challenging situations.

It's amazing how music has become such an integral part of our lives. Whether we're commuting, working, or simply relaxing, music accompanies us like a friend and sets the mood.

Plants Listen to Classical Music

Classical music isn't just about the past. It's a living, breathing art form that inspires and amazes people of all ages worldwide.

Someone was curious about why birds start chirping an hour before sunrise. They discovered that the birds' chirping is a frequency that helps open up the stomata, which are tiny pores on the bottom of plant cells. This process allows plants to start breathing in the morning, acting like an alarm clock for them. The curious person found out that this frequency is also present in classical music. A farmer from the United States decided to play classical music in his cornfield, but his neighbors thought there was something wrong with him. However, when the corn grew to an impressive 15 feet tall and produced five squash per leaf, the neighbors were curious and asked him which channel the farmer was playing. The secret was classical music, which, when combined with specific plant vitamins and particular frequencies, resulted in faster growth, a phenomenon called "sonic bloom."

Music Helps Maintain Normal Blood Pressure

A study published in the journal Deutsches Arzteblatt International discovered that listening to music by Mozart and Strauss for 25 minutes positively affected blood pressure. It lowers systolic blood pressure.

A study at the University of San Diego found that listening to classical music led to a notable decrease in systolic blood pressure, compared to jazz, pop, or no music at all. Different music genres can have varying effects on blood pressure, and classical music showed a positive impact.

In other research from the Duke Cancer Institute, it was found that classical music can help reduce anxiety. During a study, men who were given headphones playing Bach concertos while undergoing a stressful biopsy showed no increase in diastolic blood pressure and reported less pain than those without music. It's incredible how classical music can create a sense of calm and ease, even in challenging situations.

So, we see, that classical music offers a plethora of advantages to listeners, and it has been cherished for centuries. Whether you're a long-time classical musician or someone curious to explore, a world of beautiful compositions is waiting for you to discover.

India has a vibrant tradition of classical music.

I would say Indian classical music is like a hidden gem in the world of music.

The classical music of India is exceptional. It is soothing, expressive, joyful, soulful, emotional and devotional.

It is said that the "Anandabhairavi" raga in Indian classical music can help maintain normal blood pressure.

Indian classical music, with its calming and soothing qualities, can help reduce stress levels. By listening to Indian classical ragas or compositions, individuals can experience a sense of tranquility, promoting relaxation and reducing stress-related symptoms. Indian classical music has been used as a complementary therapy in treating anxiety and depression. It can help alleviate symptoms, promote relaxation, and create a sense of emotional well-being.

Plants respond positively to Indian classical music!

An experiment was conducted to see how different types of music affect the growth of rose plants. They took 30 rose plants in separate pots and divided them into five groups. Each group listened to a different type of music—Indian Classical, Vedic chants, Western Classical, and Rock music. One group was kept in silence as a control group. They measured the shoot length, internode elongation, number of flowers, and flower diameter over 60 days. They found significant differences.

Plants exposed to Vedic chants showed the most shoot elongation, the highest number of flowers, and the largest flower diameter. Plants exposed to Indian classical music had the highest internode elongation. This means that playing Vedic chants or Indian classical music helps plants grow more than the control group or when they listen to Western classical or Rock music.

In Sanskrit, there's a saying: शिशुर्वेत्ति पशुर्वेत्ति वेत्ति गानरसं फणिः।

"*Sisurvetti pasurvetti vetti gaanarasam phanihi,*" asserts that children, animals, and snakes comprehend and respond to the nectar of music. Given the results of experiments on plants, I think plants could also be included in this saying.

Music helps students and professionals

Music can have a powerful effect on one's mindset and concentration.

It is said that the great Indian cricketers Sachin Tendulkar and Rahul Dravid found a source of focus and inspiration in Carnatic music before hitting the cricket field.

A study conducted at a university in France found that students who listened to classical music during a one-hour lecture performed better on a quiz about the lecture compared to students who did not have music playing. The researchers believe that the music created a more vital emotional state in the students, which made them more open to absorbing the information.

Staying focused is key for students to do well in their studies. Listening to music boosts concentration and productivity. Whether you're studying, working, or simply trying to find Indian classical music, it can be your trusty companion to help you stay in the zone. Also, it can positively influence cognitive functions, including attention, memory, and problem-solving.

Reduction in Anxiety and Depression Symptoms: Indian Classical compositions are known for their calming and soothing effects. Many people experience high stress levels due to various reasons, such as working from home or the office, demanding work environments, long hours, tight deadlines, and the pressure to meet expectations and excel in their careers. Financial concerns, such as debt, living expenses, job insecurity, and the pursuit of financial stability, can be a source of stress for individuals and families. Listening to Indian classical music can help relax the mind and body, reducing stress and promoting a sense of tranquility.

Nada Yoga

Indian classical music is known as Nada yoga, a practice that aids in attaining self-realization and elevating human consciousness. Indian classical music has fixed melodic structures called "Ragas," which are unique. Ragas are like the stars in the sky, which can evoke different emotions, and they are meditative.

Music therapy techniques, such as guided listening or engaging in musical activities, can help individuals explore and express their emotions, improve self-awareness, and develop coping mechanisms.

It was discovered that the COVID pandemic yielded more significant shifts in mood compared to these other situations.

Many Indian classical musicians shared their joy of singing on social media during COVID. This is a great indication that the music community plays a significant role in alleviating problems in society by uplifting the moods of stressed individuals.

Ragas Can Put You To Sleep

A study by researchers at the University of Toronto discovered that classical music can benefit individuals experiencing testing anxiety and insomnia. The researchers found that listening to classical music before bedtime helped people with sleep difficulties fall asleep more quickly and stay asleep longer. By tuning into classical music, individuals can soothe their minds and promote better sleep.

Music sages in deep meditation have discovered Indian classical music which produces a calming and soothing effect. Many people find that listening to gentle classical raga pieces before bed can create a peaceful atmosphere that facilitates more restful sleep. For example, a lullaby in Neelambari raga can make you sleep. Ragas like Sankarabharanam help slow down the heart rate, regulate breathing, and promote a sense of serenity, facilitating the transition into sleep.

Research suggests that exposure to classical music, particularly compositions with repetitive patterns, can aid in language development including speech perception, vocabulary acquisition, and fluency.

Is someone addicted to bad habits? One of the great musicians once said, "*Get high on Indian classical music. That's enough.*"

According to a Yoga guru, Indian music has the potential to heal even incurable diseases. He said music can activate the Ajna chakra, the mysterious "third eye", also known as the wisdom eye.

The melodic compositions, known as ragas, are designed to create a harmonious and peaceful atmosphere. So, if you're feeling a little stressed or overwhelmed, immersing yourself in the serene sounds of Indian classical music can be like a musical retreat for your soul.

Remember, Indian classical music is like a musical treasure chest filled with endless possibilities.

Whether you're seeking relaxation, an improved focus, an emotional upliftment, or a way to express yourself, it's there to accompany you on your journey.

For example, try listening to the raga "Hamsadhwani," where the melodic tones capture the calm and peaceful essence of a swan's graceful demeanor. Ragas like "Saama" induce a peaceful state, while the "Mohana" raga improves focus, and the raga "Kadanakutuhalam" inspires soldiers to fight the battle. The "Todi" ragam, with its soothing komala swaras, reduces aggression and fosters compassion. For those struggling with depression, the "Kalyani" raga, with its uplifting tivra swaras, aids in returning to a positive and hopeful state.

My friend, why not explore the beauty of Indian classical music? You don't need to know the ragas to enjoy it. Just listen to the enchanting sounds, discover your favorite ragas, and let the Indian Music bring you peace and inspiration.

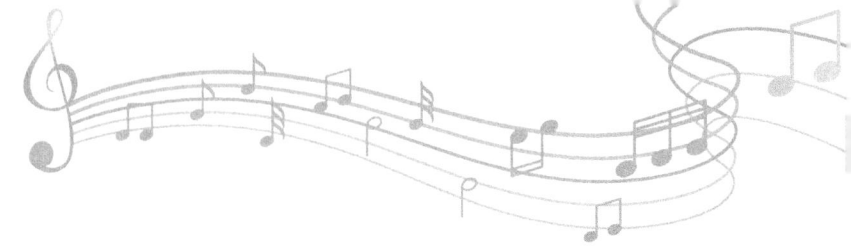

CHAPTER 2

SINGING STONES

"Follow the whispers of the tides, and you shall find the answers you seek."

*I*ntrigued by the mysterious message, I felt an irresistible pull toward Indian music.

With each step in the sand, I embrace the raga-infused soil beneath me.

The three oceans bring sands of different colors—yellow, black, and even red. Because of their distinct grain sizes, the various colors don't blend, resulting in each wave forming a unique pattern on the beach. I remember visiting the same place during my school excursion when I was in eighth grade. I had <u>brought</u> small packs of the three different colors of sand, and I was really excited.

Bhaarat, synonymous with India, evokes thoughts of "Bharata", the land of music. "Bharata" is interpreted as "Bhava, Raga, Tala"—where "Bha" stands for "Bhava"(emotion), "Ra" stands for "Raga" (melody) and "Ta" stands for "Tala" (rhythm). The land of music has a deep-rooted music tradition, which is diverse and complex. I feel that the bhava, raga, tala are not new to Indians. It is inherent in the flow of life of the people.

I worship the Triveni Sangam of bhava, raga, and tala, which is evident in the rising sun of Indian music. The magical land has witnessed one of the most complex music systems in the world.

Indian music features 108 types of beat patterns called "Taala" that you won't find in any other musical tradition in the world.

Boats float rhythmically on the shiny waves of the sea.

The location at Kanyakumari is called Triveni Sangam, a place of such sanctity that a bath in its waters is believed to cleanse away all sins. I take a dip in the Ganges of Indian music. The colorful sun shines on the ragas, the core of Indian music. The morning breeze, "Malayamarutam", whispers shruti.

"Sa- Ri - Ga- Ma" Pillars at Vijaya Vittala Temple, Hampi

I pick the musical seashells on the shore, and they whisper "SA RI GA MA PA DA NI" in my ears. The enchanting beauty of the musical pillars at the Vijaya Vittala temple in Hampi, India, lingers in my heart.

One fascinating connection between music and architecture can be found in the temples of India. In particular, the Vijaya Vittala temple in Hampi, Karnataka- a UNESCO World Heritage site, holds a special allure. These temples were not just places of worship but also spaces where music played a vital role.

Renowned for its architectural beauty and the unparalleled craftsmanship of ancient artisans, the Vijaya Vittala temple is a dedicated sanctuary to Lord Vishnu.

Among its remarkable features, the music pillars are a testament to the temple's grandeur. These pillars possess the extraordinary ability to produce musical tones when gently tapped with a thumb or a sandal stick found within the Maha Mandapa pavilion; the temple boasts 56 such music pillars, often referred to as the "singing stones" or "sa-re-ga-ma pillars." In Indian classical music, these pillars are named after the seven musical notes: SA, RI, GA, MA, PA, DA, and NI, collectively known as the "Saptaswara."

Ragas, the building blocks of Indian music, consist of a combination of notes. In both Hindustani and Carnatic classical music traditions of Indian music, the seven basic notes are known as Sa, Ri (or Re), Ga, Ma, Pa, Dha, and Ni. These notes are also referred to as Sargam in Indian classical music. They are analogous to Western musical notes. The seven swaras, originating from India, are said to have been the source of inspiration to the Western world thousands of years ago.

My thoughts delve into the origin of these notes. The first note, SA, is referred to as "Shadja." In Sanskrit, "shat" means six, and "ja" means "born out of." Shadja signifies that the other six notes are derived from SA, the first note.

Sangeetha Maharshis, the sages of India, discovered these notes. Each note is believed to have originated from different sources:

- SA (Shadjam) – originated from the peacock
- RI (Rishabham) – originated from the ox
- GA (Gandharam) – originated from the goat
- MA (Madhyamam) – originated from the Krouncha pakshi (a celestial bird from heaven)
- PA (Panchamam) – originated from the cuckoo
- DA (Daivatam) – originated from the horse
- NI (Nidhadam) – originated from the elephant

Inside the Vijaya Vittala temple, every pillar is said to be individually tuned to these "sa ri ga ma" notes of the Indian music scale, creating a soothing melody for offering prayers to the gods. I feel the enchanting music of evening concerts echoing through the Vijaya Vittala Temple.

It led me into deep contemplation, wondering about the ragas played by those pillars.

At the heart of Indian music lies the philosophy of raaga. Indian classical music finds its essence in the concept of Raaga, a profound form of melody constructed on a structured framework. A Raga is made up of Swara (musical note). Raga is derived from a melakarta, which is equivalent to a scale in Western music. Just as a tree cannot exist without a seed, Indian classical music cannot exist without the presence of Raaga. The essence of the entire world of Indian classical music revolves around ragas, which are akin to flowers offered with devotion to God.

Indian classical music encompasses two popular styles: Hindustani and Carnatic. The southern Indian style is called Carnatic music (Carnatic classical music) or the South Indian classical music, while the northern Indian style follows the Hindustani music tradition. Both styles have their distinct renditions based on ragas, which serve as the pillars of their respective musical traditions. Ragas are centered around compositions in South Indian classical music called Carnatic music, shine like stars in the sky of ananya bhakti, devotion.

Some pillars at Vijaya Vittala temple are even crafted to produce woodwind-like sounds, while others emulate traditional Indian musical instruments such as the Veena.

The harmonious notes of these pillars blend with the reverberations of percussion instruments such as the mridangam and ghatam, crafting a divine symphony of expression.

The craftsmanship behind these music pillars remains shrouded in mystery, leaving us in awe of the ancient artisans' skills and ingenuity.

The musical pillars of the Vijaya Vittala temple transport us back in time, serving as a testament to the rich cultural heritage and artistic mastery of South India.

Carnatic music flourished during the reign of the Vijayanagar Empire (1336–1565), centered in South India. I offer my salutations to the kings, musicologists, and composers who illuminated Carnatic music.

A radiant light touched the waves, poured a cool breeze, and the gentle melody of the ocean's "Sa Ri Ga Ma Pa Da Ni..." octave resonated softly in my ears.

These Indian musical notes are indeed a marvel of the world. There is no need for doubt when ancient texts affirm that the influence of the ancient Indian music book, "Naradiya Siksha," is seen in Greek music.

The widespread waves reaching the beach resembled an elaborate raga alapana, as if the sea's melody originated from the abyss of its muladhara, inviting me to be a part of the timeless narrative of Indian music, culture, and heritage.

A saint with saffron robes, blowing a conch at the shore reminded me of

ॐ अग्निमीळे पुरोहितं यज्ञस्य देवमृत्विजम् ।
होतारं रत्नधातमम्

Om Agnimlille Purohitam Yajnyasya Devam-Rtvijam |

Hotaaram Ratna-Dhaatamam

This means, *"I adore Agni (fire), the purohita (priest) of sacrifice, the provider of the treasure of knowledge."* Mythologically, the saffron color symbolizes "Sandhya," which means sunset as well as sunrise, and pays respects to the god Agni.

The sunset at Triveni Sangamam poured its light into the sea. The awakening notes of the Bhupala raga are ready to wake up the other side of the globe, with their sweet, mellifluous tune.

CHAPTER 3

PRANAVA NAADA – OM

I closed my eyes as I entered the meditation hall at Vivekananda Rock. The soul dives deep, immersed in the meditation of OM. The beauty of meditation at the southernmost tip of India is splendid and beyond description. The morning atmosphere at Vivekananda Rock is so calm and serene that it naturally guides an aspirant into a tranquil silence. After some time in my meditation, I opened my eyes, greeted by a smile.

In my childhood, I heard a story about Swami Vivekananda. He had reached Kanyakumari in 1892 after a challenging journey from Kolkata in 1888. In a daring feat, he jumped into the sea, swimming alone towards the rock, bravely challenging the relentless waves. After three days and nights of deep meditation, Vivekananda returned to consciousness.

I recollect, that when I was young I had the opportunity to experience guided meditation led by a wonderful teacher Subhash Patriji. He discovered Pyramid Meditation, which involves meditating inside a pyramid. This practice, known as Pyramid Meditation, can evoke various feelings, from calmness to intense euphoria, for many participants.

I am silent for a while, thinking of silence alone. I think music is not so different from silence. The real music beautifies the quiet moments and moves the soul, leading to ultimate bliss. Real music has a pause of silence that enhances the essence of the song.

Silence in music is like giving your stomach a little pause after enjoying tasty pani puri and waiting for your turn to get the filling of mashed potato, and chickpeas for the next round of pani puri!

There exists a component called "Anahata nada" – It is considered as the inner sound that is not produced by any external source, but rather resonates within oneself. "Anahata" means unstruck or unhurt, and "Nada" means sound.

I realize that the sound of our inhaling and exhaling produces the "So" and "ham." If we observe it repeatedly, it turns into "HamSa."

"Om" originated from "Hamsa." The "SO" "HAM" transform into the essence of O and M, creating the sacred Om or Pranava. Embrace this sound with each breath, and liberate yourself from the cycle of birth and death. This practice, known as Pranavopasana, is highly recommended in the Vedas.

Hamsa resembles a swan which serves as a vehicle of gods. Hamsa symbolizes higher spiritual knowledge. It represents Om. According to Rig Veda, the bird can separate Soma from water when they're mixed together. In later Indian writings, it separates milk from water when mixed together.

The Hamsa Upanishad is a Sanskrit text where Hindu sage Gautama talks with the divine Sanatkumara. They discuss Hamsa-vidya, which is a crucial aspect to grasp, before learning Brahmavidya. The text explains the connection between Om and Hamsa and how meditating on it helps with the journey to understanding Paramahamsa. The Hamsa mantra signifies "I am He."

It strikes me that Muthuswamy Dikshitar's father, Ramaswamy Dikshitar, created the raga "Hamsa Dhwani" inspired by the rhythmic breath ("HamSa") and the Hamsa Upanishad. This raga is associated with Lord Ganesh due to the iconic composition "Vatapi Ganapatim Bhaje."

Maybe the composer picked "Hamsadhwani" raga because Lord Ganesha represents the five life forces (pancha prana). The "Hamsadhwani" raga has five music notes, and the note "Antara Gandhram" (Ga) is often called the God note because it usually doesn't need musical embellishments (gamaka). The note shines, and the song starts with the Ga note.

In this kriti, Muthuswamy Dikshitar says, "Pranavaswaroopa vakrathundam". Lord Ganesha is attracted to Om. Lord Ganesha is the god of Muladhara Chakra.

At the base of the spine rests the Muladhara, housing the dormant serpent power. The seeker directs their focus towards consciousness and the mind, awakens Kundalini to rise through the six chakras, and reach Sahasrara, the thousand-petaled lotus at the crown of the head. Understanding the Muladhara itself is believed to grant liberation.

AUM

The symbol "OM" glowed in front of me.
I discovered the four speech stages (Vak) while researching the "Vatapi Ganapathim" song. These are Para, Pashyanti, Madhyama, and Vaikhari. Para is the first stage, an inaudible sound in the Muladhara. In this stage, there's no stress for speaking. The second stage is

Pashyanti, where there's a little stress in the Manipura Chakra. Madhyama is the third stage, reached at the Anahata Chakra, where the sound is about to form. Vaikhari is the last stage when an audible sound is heard, and people only speak at this stage. There are two kinds of sounds in yoga: the heard (Ahata) and the unheard (Anahata).

Om is the essence of all Vedas. The soil soaked with spirituality witnessed the most potent sound, "Om."

Naada, the celestial sound, encompasses the constant OM sound that resonates in meditation. Renowned Indian music composer Tyagaraja beautifully expresses, "*O mind! Drink the nectar called raga, which manifests as ‹Naadomkara swara'—raga is indeed in the form of naada and Aum (OM).*"

The ancient Indian text Bhagavad Gita declares, "*oṁ ityekākṣharaṁ brahma*" — OM represents the primordial sound that emerged as the first sound in the universe. OM consists of three syllables: A, U (pronounced as "Oh"), and M. It is believed that chanting AUM can stimulate three chakras. In yoga, the life force energy known as "prana" traverses the body, radiating energy through the seven chakras. The musical seven notes can influence the seven chakras. When you produce the sound "Ah" from your belly, you feel the vibrations in your stomach. When you vocalize "Ohh," the vibrations resonate in your throat. Finally, when you utter "Mm," you sense the vibrations in your forehead. These correspond to the Manipura and Ajna chakras.

The "O" sounds like the "a" sound within the word "saw," combined with the "u" sound within the phrase "put." Blend the "m" into the top. These sounds should all merge into one sound like the "ome" in "home."

1. Get ready to make the sound "U" with your mouth.
2. Keep your mouth in the same position and start saying "AUM". You'll feel a deep "O" sound coming from your throat.
3. Finish by humming "M" deeply.
4. Sit up straight and close your eyes.
5. Take a nice, long, deep breath in and let it out.
6. With your next deep breath, let out a low "Ooooo" sound from your belly.
7. When you're halfway through your breath, slowly close your lips into an "Mmmmmmmmm" sound.
8. Then, gradually stop and enjoy the quiet.
9. That's one "Om!" You can do as many as you want.

The Chanting of Om (Pranava Japa) for some time tremendously influences the mind. It generates harmonious vibrations and elevates the mind to divine splendor.

Om is called Udgitha and should be meditated for fearlessness and immortality.

Composer Tyagaraja Swamy states, "*Prananala samyogamu valana.. Prananadamu..*" in his kriti "Mokshamu galada." In this kriti, he states that music with Pranava or Om bestows moksha(liberation). Prana vibrates, moves the air, generates heat, and strikes the vocal cords, and the sound is produced. According to Upanishads, Om is associated with prana. Through OM, the great sages attained Nirvikalpa Samadhi, the knowledge of self.

All musical notes, all words, all the sentences, all the sounds, and all the languages emanate from Om.

It is said that different sounds like buzzing bees, musical instruments like the mridangam and ghatam, the roar of lions, the hissing of cobras, and even the clapping of people come from a sound called "Om."

Lord Krishna holds the flute because the flute represents Om. Lord Krishna tells his devotees to let go of pride and have a pure mind. He suggests that we can find peace by focusing on Om and meditating on it. The beautiful music that touches our hearts comes from Om, and it brings a sense of lasting peace.

Omkareshwar temple of lord shiva (Lord of Omkara) is located in Madhya Pradesh. It is one of twelve jyotirlingas. It is said that Adi Sankara met his guru, Govinda Bhagavadpada, in a cave in this place.

Om is the voice of gurus. Patanjali says – "*Chant Om.. you will attain your goal. If nothing else works, just chant Om.*"

"*Om is described as a bow, the soul is its arrow, and Brahman is the target. It is to be done by an unerring man. One should become one with Om just like an arrow is with the bow.*" (Muṇḍaka Upaniṣad, II.ii,4) "Om" here refers to yoga. Just as the bow is the medium that leads an arrow to its target, similarly, Om is that bow that takes an individual self to Brahman.

However, the arrow can never reach its target unless it is aimed correctly. The target, i.e., Brahman should be aimed at, by the one who is free from desires to enjoy worldly objects, who is detached from everything, who has control over his senses, and has the concentration of mind.

I believe the Carnatic composer Tyagarajaswamy's composition "Nada Sudha Rasambilanu" in Aarabhi raga draws inspiration from the above-mentioned beautiful saying.

When the celestial sound "Naada" flows from the heavens, the music unfolds, originating from the ancient verses of the Vedas.

Source of Indian Classical Music

Om is the source of Vedas and scriptures such as Puranas, Upanishads, Smritis, and Darsanas. Vedas are summed up in Gayatri. Gayatri is summed up in Om. Om is said to be an omnipotent and omnipresent sound of the cosmos.

Vedic literature is organized into four sectors.

1. Rigveda – the Veda of verses
2. Yajurveda – the Veda of sacrificial texts
3. Sama Veda – the Veda of songs
4. Atharva Veda – the storehouse of dharmas, procedures of everyday life

Fire in Vedas is praised as Agni. He is said to be the son of earth (Prithvi) and the sky (Dyauh). He is the messenger between gods and human beings. Vedas praised Agni because Agni is the god of power and wealth. Fire is holy in the opinion of ancient Iranian people as well. In Vedas, fire is the mediator between humans and gods; he takes the wishes to the sky. Yagna is the performance of religious duty involving agni while chanting mantras.

While the Bhagavad Gita primarily focuses on philosophical and spiritual teachings, it does touch upon the significance of music in specific contexts. In the Bhagavad Gita, verse 10.22, it is stated:

"Vedaanam samavedosmi"

This translates to:

"I am the Samaveda amongst the Vedas."

Among the four Vedas—the Ṛig Veda, Yajur Veda, Sama Veda, and Atharva Veda—the Sama Veda holds a special place. It specifically highlights the divine glories and attributes of God. The Sama Veda is known for its melodic nature and is sung in reverence to the Supreme Lord.

Saamaveda is the Rig Veda itself rewritten as the musical notes. Saamaveda is demonstrated. It can not be discussed. Samadeva has a tune and rhythm that adds glory to it because it is tied up in musical notes. Samaveda is described as Akasena Vihamgam Like watching birds flying in the sky. Just like a bird glides effortlessly through the air, it's like a fish that moves smoothly in the water.

The Sama Veda is one of the four sacred texts of Sanatan dharma, and it is associated with musical chants and melodies. It is believed that the Sama Veda contains songs that were sung during ancient Vedic rituals and ceremonies. These chants were considered a form of spiritual practice and a way to connect with the divine. The commencement of Brihat Sama involves the rendering of the sacred sound, Om. Om becomes the base note "shadja" in the sruti. All the other notes are created by Shadja. Hence, every note is Om in the musical scale.

Indian classical music has its roots in the Vedas. Initially, Rigveda was sung with only two notes. As time passed, the singing of the Veda progressed to include three notes. Eventually, this evolved into singing Rigveda using 4, 5, 6, and 7 notes. The evolution of "Samagana Murchana" is akin to the Kharahara Priya raga. In that era, this particular musical form was also referred to as the Chitta Ranjani raga. Later, it became Kharaharpriya raga.

The sages are called "rishis" who discovered music in deep meditation. The music in India is called "sangeet", which is known as the Indian classical music in modern times.

Naadopasana

The Sanskrit words "Naada" means sound or tone, and "Upasana" means worship or meditation.

Indian classical music is called "Naada vidya." Sound is the basis of Nadopasana embracing the naada. Learning Indian classical music is regarded as Nadopasana, a divine practice that holds the nectar of naada, the celestial sound that resonates with devotion. Naada, the musical vibrations, permeate the ears and manifest as the life force, prana vayu, flowing from the heart (hridaya sthana) to the cosmic aperture, Brahmarandhra.

Naada is believed to originate from the elements of space (akasa) and air (vayu), fanned by the fire (Agni) that resides above the abdomen, ascending towards the countenance, reflecting its influence on the face.

Vayu
|
Vahni (Agni)
|
Mind
|
Atma

According to this understanding, the soul (Atma) within the body guides and prompts the mind, which in turn stimulates the fire (agni), and the fire activates the air (vayu). As the air travels, it transforms into sound, starting from the root chakra (mooladhara) passing through the naval (naabhi), heart (hridaya), throat (kantha), crown (sirasu), and finally reaching the face (mukham).

"The Song of Sannyasin," a stanza collection of poems, was composed by Swami Vivekananda.

The first poem is as follows:

Wake up the note! the song that had its birth

Far off, where worldly taint could never reach

In mountain caves and glades of forest deep

Whose calm no sigh for lust or wealth or fame

Could ever dare to break; where rolled the stream

Of knowledge, truth, and bliss that follows both

Sing high that note, Sannyasin bold! Say -

"Om Tat Sat, Om!"

This means – Let's take inspiration from the teachings of scriptures such as the Bhagavad Gita and Upanishads, which can act as a guide helping us to be better, happier people.

The meeting point of the Bay of Bengal, Arabian Sea, and Indian Ocean is a sacred bathing place known as the Triveni Sangam. Bathing at Kanyakumari beach is often referred to as a "three sea bath" experience.

I feel that the same experience can be felt upon listening to the music of the carnatic trinity. The Carnatic music Trinity – Tyagaraja, Muthuswamy Dikshitar, and Syama Sastri worshiped "naadopasana," delving deeply into the understanding of OM (naada). Legendary composers composed songs based on the vast knowledge of ragas, Indian scriptures, and "Navavidha bhakti" – the nine types of bhakti, and the "path of devotion."

My mind is calmly enjoying the music of the waves which has an inherent rhythm.

It is said that true meditation is learning to keep our minds silent. When we surrender ourselves to the supreme consciousness, we find answers, and peace fills our hearts.

CHAPTER 4

VRINDAVAN MELLOWS

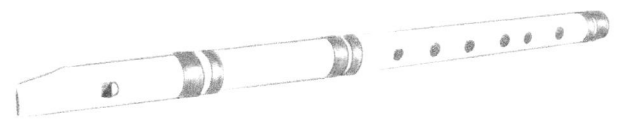

*A*midst the bustling streets of Kanyakumari, I found myself enveloped in a whirlwind of colors, sounds, and smells. As I navigated through the vibrant chaos of the marketplace, a soft, melodious tune caught my attention. Following the enchanting sound, I discovered a lone flutist seated near the shore, his fingers dancing effortlessly over the bamboo instrument.

The flute, or venu, is a wind instrument with a sweet and melodic sound. The flute is also called

"Bansuri". The word "Bans" means bamboo. Craftsmen in Kumbakonam, Tamil Nadu, are renowned for their skill in crafting flutes. The bamboo used to make these flutes is sourced from Nagercoil and Coimbatore. There exist many tales surrounding the flute.

Ustad Experiences the God of Music

Ustad Bismillah Khan, the maestro of the Shehnai, once experienced a divine encounter with Bhagwan Shri Krishna, transcending religious boundaries. Despite being a devout Muslim, the legendary musician held immense affection, respect, and Bhakti for Bhagwan Shri Krishna, prompting a mystical meeting.

This extraordinary event unfolded during Ustad Bismillah Khan's train journey from Jamshedpur to Varanasi many years ago. Seated in the third-class compartment of a coal-run passenger train, he shared the space with a young cowherd boy who boarded at an intermediate rural station. Dark and slender, the boy held a flute and soon began playing enchanting melodies.

The maestro, unfamiliar with the "Raga" being played, was captivated by the exceptional quality of the music. According to Ustad Bismillah Khan, this young musician was none other than Bhagwan Shri Krishna himself, the Supreme God.

As the divine music flowed from Krishna's flute, Ustad's heart swelled with ecstasy, experiencing the divine essence of Nada-Brahman. Tears of joy welled up in his eyes, moved by the celestial performance. After the enchanting recital, Ustad approached the young Krishna, offering coins and requesting him to play again. Bhagwan Shri Krishna obliged, continuing until Ustad's wallet was emptied. Krishna disembarked at the next station, disappearing into the divine realms.

Ustad Bismillah Khan was en route to a music concert related to the Kumbha Mela, where he introduced the new "Raga" learned from Krishna. Enamored by the melodic "raga," the audience implored Ustad to perform it repeatedly. When questioned by music scholars about the name of the "Raga," Bismillah Khan revealed it to be "Kanharira," a gift from the divine encounter with Bhagwan Shri Krishna.

Bhagawan Sri Krishna carried the flute, and some stories are associated with the flute.

The Transformation of Bamboo

Every day, Lord Krishna would venture into the enchanting forests of Vrindavan, immersing himself in playful activities beneath the serene canopy of trees. The trees revealed the joy of his presence, forming a sacred bond with the divine being. However, on a particular day, Krishna entered the forest with a troubled countenance.

Observing his distress, a curious bamboo tree gently inquired, "Krishna, what troubles you? Why do you appear so concerned?" With a solemn expression, Krishna responded, "I have something to ask of you." With unwavering devotion, the bamboo assured, "Ask, Krishna, and whatever you request, I shall willingly comply."

Lord Krishna revealed his desire with a heavy heart, saying, "Dear bamboo, I wish to cut you into pieces." The bamboo, displaying unwavering faith, queried, "Is that truly your wish?" Krishna affirmed, "Yes, it is a task I must undertake." Without hesitation, the bamboo consented, prepared to endure the impending separation.

Krishna wielded his divine hands, and the bamboo cried out in pain as it was meticulously crafted into pieces. However, from this apparent agony emerged something extraordinary—a magnificent flute that echoed with the essence of Krishna's divine breath.

Lord Krishna carried his newfound creation flute, with him, everywhere, captivating the hearts of all who heard the enchanting melodies. The gopis, in their admiration, couldn't help but express their envy and questioned the bamboo, "How do you manage to stay with god all the time?"

In response, the bamboo humbly revealed its wisdom, "I remain close to the divine because I am empty from within. Lord Krishna's breath infuses me with purpose, creating beautiful ragas and tunes. I surrender to him with grace, allowing his divine presence to resonate through me." And so, the bamboo stood as a testament to the transformative power of surrender and emptiness in the presence of the divine.

Flute and the Five Elements

Bamboo shoots, rooted in the Earth and nourished by water, absorb the breath of fire, creating enchanting music when played. The resulting melodies travel through the air and seem to merge with the sky. The flute, as an instrument, beautifully incorporates all five elements.

Krishna Refuses to Play the Flute

Once Krishna left Vrindavan and went to Madhura. To everyone's surprise there, he had stopped playing his flute altogether. Somehow, the people of Madhura had also discovered the enchanting tunes of his flute. People who were close to him wanted to hear the sweet melodies of his flute, so they asked him to play. However, Krishna declined their request.

Lord Krishna told them, "If you want to hear the flute, you must go to Vrindavan. The gopis there have absorbed my music so well that it's like meditation for them. They carry my tunes in their hearts, and their thoughts, words, actions, and songs are all filled with Krishna (Krishnamayam). If you go there and pay attention, you'll hear my flute."

Lord Krishna Talks about Gopis in Vrindavan

One day, Uddhava asked Lord Krishna, "Why are the gopis so special? What makes them stand out among all your devotees?" Krishna replied, "All my devotees are precious to me, no doubt. But the gopis hold a special place. While other devotees may shed tears upon hearing my name, the gopis go a step further. For them, every name they hear is like my name. When they listen to music, they imagine it as my flute playing. And every color they see reminds them of me. It's these special connections that make the gopis dear to my heart."

Krishna and the Peacock Feather

Once upon a time, the peacocks approached Lord Krishna with a special request: to play his flute for them. Krishna, with a kind heart, began playing mesmerizing melodies on his flute, and the peacocks responded joyfully by dancing to the enchanting tunes. The lively dance went on for hours, with the peacocks thoroughly immersed in the sheer delight of Krishna's flute.

When the dance concluded, the King of the peacocks expressed deep gratitude to Lord Krishna and offered a beautiful peacock feather as a token of appreciation. In his gracious manner, Krishna accepted the feather and placed it on his head as a symbol of honor. And that, they say, is why we often see peacock feathers adorning Lord Krishna's head.

Power of Sarabha Shastry's Music

There used to be a flutist, Sarabha Sastrigal, a skilled musician who was born in Kumbakonam, Tamilnadu, in 1872. When he lost his sight at the tender age of two, his father was deeply worried about his son's future.

Searching for a path to provide him with a fulfilling life, an idea struck him – music training. Before the boy even turned ten, his father crafted a flute from a bamboo stem in their backyard, creating holes for notes. As the boy put the instrument to his lips and blew, a delightful melody filled the air. Overjoyed, the father decided to teach him several exercises. The young boy, blessed with natural talent and a sharp mind, progressed swiftly. Later, under the guidance of Manambuchavadi Venkatasubbayyar, a disciple of Saint Tyagaraja he learned Tyagaraja's kritis and swiftly gained fame. Even as a boy, he began performing, showcasing his exceptional musical abilities. Later he became a great vidwan and exponent of flute.

Sarabha Sastri had a unique ability. Whenever he played the Punnagavarali raga, snakes would emerge from their hiding spots and dance to his music.

Once, he agreed to perform at a wedding. As he began playing his flute, the bride, who had heard a lot about Sastrigal's talent, couldn't help but laugh at the small instrument he held. This hurt Sastrigal's feelings, but he didn't let it show.

Toward the end of the concert, he decided to play the Punnagavarali raga. Suddenly, a cobra slithered into the hall spread its hood, and started dancing to the music. The audience was amazed and a bit scared. Someone quietly informed Sastrigal about the snake.

Undeterred, he continued playing the raga, reaching a climactic moment before gently concluding it. Miraculously, the snake, satisfied by the music, retreated without causing harm to anyone. The incident left the audience in awe of Sastrigal's extraordinary connection with the enchanting power of his music.

Tirumarugal Natesa Pillai, the renowned Nadaswara expert, enjoyed listening to Sastrigal's music. Once, he was scheduled to perform in the Parthasarathy Swamy temple procession in Triplicane, Madras. However, as the procession reached Singarachari Street, someone informed him that Sastrigal's flute concert was happening nearby. Quickly, he handed his Nadaswaram to his assistant and instructed his assistant to continue playing, pretending he would return in a few minutes. He went to the flute concert and became engrossed in the enchanting music of Sarabha Sastrigal, completely forgetting about his prior commitment. As the Deity's procession approached the temple, his companions rushed to him and brought him back. He then resumed playing the Nadaswaram, completing the performance as originally planned.

Sarabha Sastri's flute remains on exhibit, to this day, at Sri Rama Bhajanai Sabha in Kumbakonam, carefully preserved by his family members.

Mali's Flute

Tiruvidaimarudur Ramaswamy Mahalingam (1926–1986) "Mali" was a revered flutist who transformed the approach to flute-playing in Carnatic music.

According to his disciple Sundaram, Mali believed he could perceive God within five minutes of playing. He considered it meaningless to continue beyond that point and would stop.

Mali took pleasure in presenting his accompanists with intricate musical progressions, relishing the challenge. You can enjoy his performances, particularly the melodious renditions of Kaapi, Todi, Kalyani, Begada, and Kambhoji ragas, online on YouTube.

N. Ramani, a renowned flutist, was mentored by the master flutist Mali. Ramani always acknowledged the immense wisdom and skill of his guru, Mali. He believed that a truly good teacher remains receptive to learning from their students as well. Interestingly, Mali himself learned the Aahiri raga from Ramani, who had acquired it from T. Viswanathan, the brother of the legendary dancer Balasaraswathi. As I reminisced about Flute Mali's rendition of the Ahiri raga, its sweet haunting melody enveloped the night skies of Kanyakumari.

CHAPTER 5

TIRUVARUR CONNECTION

I began my trip from the bottom of India, Kanyakumari, where the land meets three seas. I'm ready to drive north through Tamil Nadu in my car to visit Lord Shiva temple known as Tyagaraja Swamy temple at Tiruvarur. Thiruvarur is renowned as the birthplace of the musical legends Tyagaraja Swamy, Muthusamy Dikshithar, and Shama Sastry.

The sun was rising as I left Kanyakumari in my car, excited to explore Tamil Nadu's historic places like Tiruvarur. I traveled in my car along the road, feeling the cool breeze. Every mile I drove felt like a new part of a story, with temples and interesting things waiting for me.

I followed the map to go to Tiruvarur. After driving for about eight hours through Madurai city, the air felt different as I got closer to Tiruvarur.

People believe that being born in Thiruvarur helps one attain freedom from the cycle of birth and death.

Also, if someone passes away in Varanasi, it is believed that they will attain spiritual liberation called Moksha. Worship in Chidambaram or meditating on Arunachalam (Tiruvannamalai) is also believed to lead to Moksha. Certain temples symbolize spiritual knowledge. The Tiruvarur temple, along with the sacred site known as Kamalalaya, embodies the highest Advaitic wisdom, referred to as Hamsa Vidya. In Indian philosophy, "Hamsa" holds significant symbolism. It represents the divine swan, often associated with higher consciousness and spiritual purity.

Tyagaraja Swamy temple is associated with names of saivites like Appar and Sundarar. In his Tevaram works, Sundarar, an 8th-century Saivite saint, expresses his devotion: "I am the servant of all those born in Thiruvarur."

The world of Carnatic music witnessed the rise of a remarkable trio, often hailed as the Trinity of Carnatic music in the 18th century.

Thiruvarur is the birthplace of the Trinity of Carnatic music: Tyagaraja, Muthuswami Dikshitar, and Syama Sastri. In their era, these three luminaries emerged as both composers and visionaries who would sculpt a new epoch in the rich tapestry of Carnatic music.

With their unparalleled prowess in music, the Trinity reshaped the very essence of Carnatic music, leaving an indelible mark on its history. Their collective genius brought about a transformative wave, challenging and redefining the existing traditions of

Carnatic music. Their efforts enriched the South Indian musical landscape.

When it came to creating songs, each had a unique style. Muthuswami Dikshitar loved using the Sanskrit language in his compositions. Meanwhile, Tyagaraja and Syama Sastri preferred writing their songs mostly in Telugu. Their choice of languages added a special flavor to their music, making each of them stand out in their own way.

Saint Tyagaraja

Tyagaraja is one of the iconic composers of South Indian classical music. He was named after Thyagaraja, Lord Shiva.

Saint Tyagaraja was a great devotee of Lord Rama. He composed most of the compositions on Lord Rama. Lord Rama woke up with the songs of Tyagaraja and slept when he sang a lullaby. He was a naada yogi, an enlightened musician. He composed soul-stirring and highly inspiring devotional songs. He composed thousands of songs; however, only around 800 compositions are available today. Tyagaraja Swamy reveals a treasure of music knowledge called "Swararnavam" known to Lord Shiva. Lord Shiva had shared the knowledge with his better half, Parvati Devi.

Because of Lord Shiva's compassion, ragas are known to the music world. Legend has it that the sage Narada appeared before Tyagaraja Swamy and gifted him the book "Swararnava." Overwhelmed with joy and devotion, Tyagaraja started singing with great ecstasy and expressed his gratitude by composing numerous songs dedicated to Narada.

Tyagaraja used to live in Tiruvarur, the serene town in Thanjavur district. His inclination towards spirituality led him on a remarkable journey.

One day, a bhagavatottama (sage) from Kanchipuram visited Tiruvarur. The news of the saint's presence spread like wildfire, and people from all around flocked to seek his blessings. Tyagaraja, too, felt a magnetic pull toward the saint and decided to pay his respects.

In the presence of the revered sage, Tyagaraja found solace and wisdom. With a gentle smile, the saint shared a profound secret of attaining spiritual liberation. He declared that whoever chants the divine name of Rama for 96 crores times will achieve jivanmukta—a state of liberation while still living—and ultimately attain God.

This revelation filled Tyagaraja's heart with boundless joy. Determined to embark on this sacred journey, he wholeheartedly embraced the practice of chanting Rama Nama. Every day, Tyagaraja fervently chanted 1,25,000 names of Rama, immersing himself in the divine vibrations of the sacred mantra. At the tender age of twenty-one, Tyagaraja completed chanting 96 crores of Rama Nama, eventually having a vision of Rama.

Thyagaraja composed most of the songs in Telugu, a South Indian language. Telugu is the only language in the Eastern world in which every word ends with a vowel sound. In the 16th century, an Italian explorer named Niccolò de' Conti noticed that Telugu words end in vowels, similar to Italian. Because of this, he called Telugu "The Italian of the East."

There is another story. Once upon a time, a group of talented singers from India embarked on a musical journey to Italy. They were passionate about showcasing the rich heritage of Indian classical music. In the heart of Italy, they organized a mesmerizing concert featuring the timeless compositions of the renowned Indian composer Tyagaraja Swamy.

As the musicians sang the soulful melodies, their voices resonated through the Italian venue. Among the audience, an observant Italian listener was enchanted by the beauty of the words in the Telugu songs. Struck by the lyrical elegance and the rhythmic flow of the language, they found a surprising similarity between Telugu and Italian.

Intrigued by this linguistic connection, they approached the singers after the concert. They admired the musical performance and pointed out how the Telugu lyrics sounded remarkably harmonious, reminiscent of the Italian language.

Tyagaraja Swamy's compositions have influenced the sages, musicians, and lovers of music all over the world. He crafted delightful ragas like Janyatasree, captivating the world with his exquisite compositions.

Sadguru Tyagaraja Swamy's Pancharatna kritis are like five shining gems in the vast sky of Indian classical music. These songs are treasures of literary, musical, spiritual, and aesthetic values.

In the first song, "Jagadanandakaraka," set in the Naata ragam, Tyagaraja glorifies Lord Rama with 108 chantings in beautiful Sanskrit. Each chanting "Om Jagadaanandakarakaya namaha", "Om Jayaya namaha", "Om Janaki prananayakaya namaha" and so on, praises different aspects of Lord Rama's divine nature called "astottara satanamavali." Additionally, the choice of Naata ragam at the beginning symbolizes "adi naata, antya surati," indicating that Nata raga is sung initially and Surati raga at the end.

The second song, "Dudukugala," in Gowla ragam, reflects Tyagaraja's introspection on worldly desires and undesirable thoughts.

In Bhagavadgeetha, Daivasura sampad vibhag yog, Lord Krishna says to Arjun *"The divine attributes pave the path to liberation, while the demonic traits entangle one in a cycle of bondage. Do not despair, Arjun, for you are inherently having the saintly virtues."*

In this song, Tyagaraja recalls the teachings of the Bhagavad Gita.

Tyagaraja reminds us of this chapter of Bhagavadgeetha in this song. Tyagaraja is a humanist who always thought of fellow human beings and protected them from worldly desires for the welfare of society.

The third song, "Sadhinchene," in Aarabhi raga, is like a precious pendant in the necklace of five gems that inspired me to sing Carnatic music. This song captivates listeners with its electrifying effect and profound impact. It vividly portrays Lord Krishna's playful nature and mysterious conduct. Understanding the science of Lord Krishna is challenging for ordinary individuals, as he embodies eternal bliss and wisdom. Depicted with a flute in his two hands in this material world, Lord Krishna's presence is felt through the enchanting melody of Aarabhi raga, which makes us feel that the raga Aarabhi is Lord Krishna himself.

Thyagaraja's composition serves as a reminder of the teachings of the Bhagavad Gita and his humanistic approach towards societal well-being, inspiring listeners to seek paths of musical knowledge, and devotion towards god.

The fourth song, "Kanagana ruchira kanakavasana Ninnu," composed in Varali raga, renowned for its spiritual ecstasy, is a natural progression from the preceding song. Varali, meaning "bumblebee," echoes in its gamakas. I feel the buzz of the bumble bee in this song. The song's essence conveys, *"Oh Lord Rama, your darshan, divine presence illuminates us with spiritual enlightenment."*

This reminds me of the Viswaroop darshan yoga from the Bhagavad Gita, where Arjuna expresses profound joy upon witnessing the universal form of Krishna. Singing the fourth song fills us with similar elation.

The fifth song, "Endaro Mahanubhavulu," is set in Sree ragam. Sree denotes auspiciousness, Lakshmi, grace, and wealth. The musical note "Ri" adds a soft, gentle touch, enhancing the elegance of the raga. The song offers salutations to the countless noble souls, encompassing devotees of Lord Rama, saints who have achieved mastery over their minds, and those who participate in the nine types of devotion (nava vidha bhakti) to God.

Thinking of Dr. APJ Abdul Kalam, a visionary leader, scientist, India's Missile Man, and recipient of the Bharat Ratna, brings to mind his presidential oath ceremony. In his address, he expressed, "As I look before me at the distinguished dignitaries from various nations and other eminent personalities, the beautiful Tyagaraja Swamy Keertana in Sree raga resonates within my heart. "Endaro mahanubhavulu andariki vandanamulu," which means, "I salute all noble-hearted human beings."

Applause filled the air.

Tyagaraja's compositions are timeless. They are studied and cherished daily, bringing joy to millions of souls.

GuruGuha Anugraham

Muthuswamy Dikshitarwas a legendary music composer of South Indian classical music, singer and veena (a string instrument) player, who is considered one of the musical Trinity of Carnatic music along with Tyagaraja, and Syama Sastri. He composed more than 500 songs in various ragas. His compositions are blended with the spiritual treasure of knowledge of scriptures and naada vidya. One of the incidents in Muthuswamy Dikshitar's life was a turning point.

Chidambaranath Yogi, a saint scholar who initiated the Srividya cult, imparting a tantric mode of worship to Muthuswamy Dikshitar's father, was going to Varanasi back in the days. He requested that Dikshitar's father (disciple) send his son to Varnansi.

Dikshitar accompanied Chidambaranath Yogi to Varanasi. Yogi initiated Dikshitar with Srividya Upasana, taught Vedanta, propounded by Sankaracharya, and did yoga. It took a lot of work to travel to Kasi in those days. Dikshitar immersed himself in the study of Vedanta Sastra, reciting vedas, singing, and playing veena. He acquired Vedanta Shastra and music for six years in Varanasi (Kasi).

One day, the Swami called Dikshitar to the banks of the sacred Ganges. "Go down three or four steps in the Ganga" he instructed, his voice carrying affection, "and tell me what you find."

With reverence, Dikshitar obeyed his guru's command, descending the steps until the cool waters of the Ganges embraced his feet.

Dikshitar descended into the Ganga, and behold! He retrieved a Veena with the word "Rama" inscribed on it in Devanagari script. With a heart filled with gratitude, Dikshitar returned to his guru and bowed deeply. "I have found a veena, Swami," he whispered, his voice trembling with emotion.

He presented it to the Yogi. "This is the blessed offering from the Ganga Devi to you. You shall rise to become a distinguished Vedantin and Musician," declared Chidambaranatha Yogi, handing it to him along with his blessings.

My music mentor, D. K Pattammal's guru Justice T. L. Venkatrama Iyer, stated in his book that the veena is with Baluswami, the grandson of Subbarama Dikshitar, son of Ambi Dikshitar (Muthuswamy Dikshitar). Subbarama Dikshitar was not only the grandson but also the adopted son of Baluswami Dikshitar, who was a brother of Muthuswamy Dikshitar.

Muthuswamy Dikshitar was influenced by Hindustani music and introduced Hamsadhwani raga to Indian music. Dikshitar's father discovered Hamsadhwani raga.

One day Chidambarantha Yogi, while in worship before Goddess Annapurneswari, informed Dikshitar that She would provide food in this life and grant Moksha (liberation) after it. He advised Dikshitar to dedicate his entire life to worshipping Her. As they headed to the Ganga river for a bath the following day, Yogi summoned Dikshitar and expressed, "The time has come for us to part ways. Are you not eager to return home and reunite with your parents and brothers?"

Yogi left Dikshitar on the shore and proceeded, as was his routine, to immerse himself in the Ganges for a bath, marking the conclusion of his presence. He departed from this earthly realm, leaving only his lifeless body behind. The body was later recovered from the river and laid to rest in the Hanuman Ghat. Overwhelmed with sorrow at the loss of his esteemed Guru, Muthuswami Dikshitar bid farewell to Benaras and commenced his journey back home.

When Dikshitar returned to his home in Tamilnadu, he was thinking of his guru, Chidambaranatha Yogi. He remembered Yogi's ishta devata Lord Subramanya, and he would always talk about the glories of Lord Subramanya. Realizing this, Dikshitar took mandala (40 days) Deeksha at Tiruttani, an abode of Lord Subramanya. He used to do daily pooja and bhajans for forty days. On the 40th day, while Muthuswami was sitting with his eyes closed, repeating a particular mantra, something extraordinary happened.

An elderly man, full of spiritual brightness, appeared before him and said, "Muthuswami, open your mouth." Surprised, Muthuswami opened his eyes to see this wise older man. "I don't know him. How does he know my name?" wondered Muthuswami.

Then, the old man placed something in Muthuswami's mouth and said, "Close your eyes and tell me what I have given you." Muthuswami closed his eyes and said, "It is sugar candy." When he opened his eyes again, the old man had disappeared. In his place, Muthuswami saw a vision of Lord Subrahmanya sitting on a peacock with Valli and Devasena by his side. The whole scene slowly faded away, leaving Muthuswami amazed by the magical experience.

Dikshitar thought that the older man who appeared before him was Lord Subramanya, and the sugar candy given to him was like a special kind of knowledge called Gnana. He was so happy that he couldn't contain his excitement and started singing and composing music. He sang many songs praising the Lord, calling him Guru-Guha. These songs are now famous and are called Guru-Guha Kritis or sometimes the Tiruttani Kritis.

Dikshitar composed his first song, "Srinathadi Guruguhojayathi," in the Mayamalavagowla Raga set to Adi tala." Mayamalavagowla" is the first raga we learn in Carnatic Music, well associated with the Adi talam, where "Adi" also denotes the first. The song commences with notations in both arohana and avarohana (ascending and descending order of the notes), accompanied by janta swaras in its sangathis.

In this composition, "Sri" represents the beginning. The kriti is structured in the prathama vibhakti, denoting the first case in Sanskrit. In "GuruGuha," Guha means Lord Subramanya, who illuminates as the guru himself.

Raga Mayamalavagowla is believed to have associations with the borders of Bihar, Orissa, and West Bengal states of India.

Muthuswamy Dikshitar composed many songs in Sanskrit. Muthuswami's Sanskrit verses praise the temple deity yet seamlessly interweave the philosophy of Advaita into his compositions. His compositions are enriched with gamakas (modulations) and blended with the richness of Sahitya. His profound knowledge of Vedas, Vedanta, matra shastra, jyotish shastra (astrology), agamas, hindustani music, south Indian music, and veena instruments makes the compositions very special and soul-stirring. His iconic composition "Vatapi Ganapatim bhaje" in Hamsadhwani raga tells us how he influenced Indian music with the richness of raga bhava, mastery over talam (beats), and Sahitya (literature). It is said that the song reflects the teachings of the Hamsopanishad.

Dikshitar made a lot of musicians achieve eternal bliss in parabrahma by singing his compositions.

Just as one savors the sweetness and deliciousness of a ripe mango fruit, Indian music, when experienced in its true essence, provides a profound and enchanting experience that transports you into a state of supreme bliss.

The music that stirs your emotions to the point of tears is a product of the revered guru Parampara. In this grand lineage, the gurus impart the knowledge and practices to their disciples, ensuring the continuation of this sacred art form.

Every day was a sacred dawn for the Indian music seekers (disciples) as they eagerly awaited their guru's teachings on ragas.

Under the watchful guidance of their gurus in gurukulam, the disciples immerse themselves in the study of traditional music.

Blessed with innate musical talents and a deep affinity for the art, these disciples were often bestowed with great vocal abilities. In the past, musicians would undergo training in veda adhyayana, the study of the Vedas.

Gurus would carefully select disciples based on their aptitude and understanding, providing them with comprehensive training in classical music and following their own gurus' teachings in the traditional lineage.

Syama Krishna

Like his father, Syama Sastri served as the priest (archaka) in the Bangaru Kamakshi Temple in Tanjore. His parents named him "Venkata Subrahmanyan." His nickname is "Syama Krishna." This child later became "Syama Sastri," who is now known as one of the most respected composers in Carnatic music.

Their family moved to Tanjore when he was 8 years old. At the time Syama Sastri's family had the opportunity to host a monk named Sangeeta Swami, who was an expert in dance and music.

This saint who lived in Varanasi, was devoted to Lord Visweswara. He often enchanted the surroundings with his melodious songs. During his pilgrimage to Rameswaram, he passed through Tanjore.

In Tanjore, Syama Sastri's father was honored to serve this musical saint, Sangeetha Swamy. He provided him with food and showed great hospitality. One day, upon noticing young Syama Sastri, Sangeetha Swamy exclaimed to Syama's father, "This child is a musical prodigy. You must arrange good training for him."

Initially hesitant, Syama's father advised Syama Sastri that music wasn't their traditional pursuit, suggesting instead a focus on Vedanta and scriptures.

However, Sangeetha Swamy persistently urged Syama's father to nurture the boy's musical talent.

Reluctantly, Syama's father gave in, encouraging Syama to formally learn music. Syama didn't have to worry about earning a living thanks to the family's affluence. Under the guidance of the musical saint from Kasi, Syama embarked on his formal musical education.

This saint, a musical genius, shared his profound knowledge of music, passing on the nuances and intricacies to Syama. Syama diligently practiced and, being a genius himself quickly absorbed the teachings. Syama mastered the art under the saint's tutelage in just four months.

As the time came for the saint to resume his pilgrimage to Kasi, he bestowed upon Syama all his compositions, urging him to delve deeper into the world of musical bliss. The saint advised Syama to attend the concerts of the accomplished musician Adiappayyar and blessed him, declaring that Syama had the best wishes and blessings of

Goddess Kamakshi and would shine forth as one of the brightest musical gems.

Later, he learned music from Pachimiriam Adiyappayya, a famous composer of the bhairavi ata tala varnam, viriboni, and a court musician in Tanjore.

As the years went by, Syama Sastri became a well-known and respected musician, scholar, and composer. He earned admiration and respect from Tyagaraja, and it seems that the two of them often engaged in scholarly discussions.

He was a deeply devoted and sincere worshiper of Goddess Kamakshi. There are stories that he became so absorbed in prayer to the Goddess that he would lose awareness of the outside world. During these moments, he would spontaneously sing his compositions (kritis).

Syama Sastri composed various kritis on Kamakshi in Ananda bhairavi, Saveri, Kalyani and other ragas. Also, he composed swarajithis in the ragas Bhairavi, Yadukula kambhoji and Todi.

Syama Sastri's second son, Subbaraya Sastri, was also a musical prodigy. Much like his father, he composed some remarkable kritis. What makes Subbaraya Sastri unique is that he is recognized as the only individual to have learned music from Tyagaraja Swami, Muthuswami Dikshithar, and his father, Syama Sastri.

It's amazing to know someone had the great privilege of learning from the Carnatic music trinity. I felt great tranquility and peace of mind.

During my visit to the Lord Ganesha temple, I learned that Lord Ganesha is depicted in a dancing pose on a lotus with a coiled serpent, symbolizing Muladhara. This is why the place is known as Muladhara Kshetram. Muladhara refers to the Muladhara Chakra, which is said to be triangular in shape and is believed to house the dormant serpent power. When Kundalini awakens, its energy flows through various chakras until it reaches the Sahasrara, symbolized as the thousand-petaled lotus.

I went to the temple of Lord Tyagaraja. The temple tower was awe-inspiring. There was a big tree to which I bowed. I prostrated before the Holy Mast (Dhwaja Sthambham) in front of the temple. Paying homage to the Lord, I solemnly walked round "pradakshinam" surrounded by tall gopurams. The moment I saw Lord Shiva I experienced a rare joy. I folded my palms to revere Lord shiva and I prostrated before the god. I had a wonderful darshan of the main deity, Lord Shiva, known as Thyagaraja.

I bowed before the goddess Neelotpalambika. The goddess is also known as kamalambika.

I recollect that Muthuswamy Dikshitar had composed Kamalamba navavarana kritis. Muthuswami Dikshitar wrote eleven kritis known as kamalAmba navAvaraNa. These compositions praise Goddess kamalAmba at the grand Tiruvarur temple. Dikshitar's skills shine in this set, and the lyrics are exceptional!

I made my way toward the Ajapa Mandapam, drawn by the allure of its ancient walls adorned with intricate carvings that whispered tales of centuries past.

CHAPTER 6

DANCING GOD

𝒯he Lord in the temple is known as Thyagaraja, a benevolent deity who selflessly undertakes sacrifices for his devotees. I visited Ajapa Mandapam, famous for ajapa natanam, a unique dance performed every time the deity is taken out in a procession.

Muthuswamy Dikshitar composed five kritis, known as Pancha Bhuta Linga kritis, dedicated to Lord Shiva. According to the Saiva Agamas, five sacred sites in South India are known as Kshetras. At these sites, Shiva Lingas are worshipped, with each Kshetra representing one of the five elements: Kancheepuram symbolizing prithivi (earth), Jambukeswaram for aapa (water), Tiruvannamalai for teja (fire), Kalahasti for vaayu (wind), and Chidambaram for aakaasha (ether).

The temple is associated with the great devotee Sundarar, who witnessed the ajapa dance of Natesa. Lord Shiva is Nataraja, the dancing God, the cosmic dancer. When he performs "Ananda thandavam," the audience is transported to a transcendental state of bliss. He not only performs but also takes the role of the audience, delighting in his own divine performance.

As I touched the ancient pillar of Ajapa Mandapam, a rush of thoughts flooded my mind like a rushing river. When we look at the Nataraja statue, there's this radiant circle around Lord Nataraja, and it's not just a circle – it is "OM." The radiant cosmic circle is known as "jwaala maala prabha maNDala." The grand stage can encompass the entire universe or be as small as an atom.

I imagine in Kailasa, where the Himalayas touch the heavens, Lord Shiva manifests with four hands, surrounded by an eternal OM. In the heart of Mount Kailash, amidst the timeless expanse of the cosmos, a wondrous spectacle unfolded—the divine dance of Lord Shiva, the Nataraja, the cosmic dancer.

I began to sense a cosmic dance unfolding a mesmerizing concert of movement and rhythm representing the gigantic OM across the entire universe. I found myself hallucinating, where the pillars of ajapa mandapa themselves told tales of Natesha's dance concert. Nataraja is referred to as Naada Brahma, connecting the root sounds that are universal across languages.

Srusti

With the sound of the drum, Shulapani, the holder of the trident, rose from his meditative posture. In Nataraja's upper right hand, there's a drum called Dhakka or Damaru, a double-sided instrument producing a powerful rhythm. This drum symbolizes the vibration which is called "Srusti" creation, and it's suggested that the Big Bang might have originated from this cosmic drumbeat.

The glowing pranava nada painted the canvas of beautiful ragas, bringing forth drums and other musical instruments, fine-tuned themselves, setting the stage for the divine moments of the dance.

Saint composer Tyagaraja swamy's song

"Naada Tanumanisham Shankaram namami me manasa Sirasa" in Chittaranjani raga, resonated the divine Naada that flowed inside Lord Shiva, and the vara sapta swara, seven notes originating from sama veda, mesmerize the sages and drove them towards the sachidananda, the divine bliss.

I began to perceive the rhythmic pulsations of Shiva's dance, each movement imbued with profound meaning and symbolism. It was not just a dance; it was a cosmic symphony, a divine concert of movement and rhythm that reverberated throughout the cosmos.

With every step, Lord Shiva expressed the eternal cycle of creation, preservation, and destruction. His gestures spoke of the boundless power of cosmic forces, the ceaseless flow of time, and the eternal dance of life and death.

The celestial beings, from Gandharvas to Apsarases and Yakshas, stood in awe as the Lord of Dance prepared to unfold the cosmic spectacle.

Sthiti

His right hand, in the abhayahasta gesture, signifies a blessing and symbolizes a safe existence called "Sthiti."

As the sun dipped below the horizon, casting a warm glow upon the snow-capped peaks, the dance of bliss, the Ananda Tandava, awakened within him. The gods, sensing the celestial stir, gathered around with precious gems. Upon them, the Mother of the Three Worlds, Parvati, adorned with grace, sat in serene contemplation, profoundly understanding the secrets held within Swararnavam, the sacred music book that unfolded the intricacies of ragas.

Saraswati, the goddess of knowledge, plucked the strings of her veena, weaving a melody that echoed through the cosmos. Indra, the king of gods, accompanied her on the flute, creating a harmony that resonated with the heartbeat of creation. Brahma, the creator, marked the passage of time with the rhythmic clang of his cymbals.

Lakshmi, the goddess of wealth, began to sing, her voice carrying the sweetness of abundance. Vishnu, the preserver, joined the divine ensemble, playing a mridanga that echoed like the heartbeat of the universe, resonating with Tyagaraja's song "sogasuga mridanga talamu..jata gurchi ninu sokkajeyu dheerudevvado?!" The brave entertained the audience with a soulful rhythm.

The sages immersed themselves in the eternal dance of the cosmic soul reminding "Yogiraja hrudayAbja nilayam." As the music soared to celestial heights, while the king of serpents worshiped his lotus feet. "swara raga sudharasa yuta bhakti," the sweet nectar of swara, raga, and pure devotion is showered by his grace.

Samhara

In his left upper hand, Nataraja grasps the Eternal Fire, already enveloped by powerful cosmic flames called "Samhara."

I recollect Muthuswamy Dikshitars Pancha linga kriti represents Agni - अरुणाचल नाथं स्मरामि अनीशम् अपीत कुचाम्बा समेतम्। "aruṇācala nātham smarāmi anīśam apīta kucāmbā samētam" in Saranga ragam.

One of great sages Ramana Maharshi referred to Arunachala as the spiritual heart of the world. "Aruna", translating to "red, bright like fire", goes beyond mere heat-emitting flames; it represents Jnanagni, the Fire of Wisdom, neither hot nor cold. "Achala" denotes hill. Therefore, Arunachala is the "Hill of Wisdom".

Tirodhana

The position of the right leg is referred to as "sthita padam," denoting a firm foot signifying the omnipresence of the Supreme Being.

This is called "Tirodhana," a worldly attachment.

"Adenamma harudu druguta thayyani.. Amba sabashani koniyada" The lord dances cheerfully while Goddess Parvathi praises his dance. His cosmic steps left imprints on the kailash mountains. The gods, goddesses, and celestial beings watched in awe as Shiva's dance unfolded, engrossed himself in the divine music of Sama Ganam.

I recollect the kriti on Prithvi lingam (Earth), Kanchipuram in Raga Bhairavi beginning with the words

चन्तिय मा कन्द मूलकन्दं चेतःश्री सोमास्कंदं

chintaya mā kanda mūlakandam chetaḥ śrī somāskandam

This means – O mind! Meditate upon somaskanda seated under the mango tree (the linga emerged from the mango tree).

There is a suppressed demon under Nataraja's foot. This is to get rid of the evils in life.

Anugraha

The uplifted left leg reveals grace called as "Anugraha," releasing the mature soul from bondage.

The five letters signify the five actions or Pancha Krityas of the Lord, namely, Srishti (creation), Sthiti (preservation), Samhara (destruction), Tirodhana (veiling), and Anugraha (blessing). The five-lettered name of Shiva "Na mah shi va ya" came from it.

Om is the cosmic circle around him. The panchakshari evolves as Om Namah shivaya.

The smooth and gracefully extended lower left hand symbolizes spiritual upliftment. He is bestower of spiritual growth to attain liberation.

I remember a song in the Abhogi raga. The Tamil lyrics "sabhApatikku vere deivam Samanamaagumaa Thillai " convey, "Is there a god equal to lord sabhapati of Chidambaram?"

Dikshitar traveled to Chidambaram, which is one of the Pancha-Linga Kshetras. Lord Shiva is worshiped as a manifestation of Akasa (Sky). He is called Nataraja, and his cosmic dance has a mystic significance. This is one of the most famous shrines in India. I recollect the kriti in Raga Kedaram beginning with "Ananda Natana Prakasam".

आनन्द नटन प्रकाशं चित् सभेषम्
आश्रयामि शिविकामवल्लीशम्

It means "I take refuge in the lord of sivakamasundari who shines with blissful dance."

The Kedaram raga originates from the Sankarabharanam family, evoking Veera rasam. Earlier, the maestros of Nadaswaram used to perform Kedaram raga for hours.

The composition imparts a profound sense of satisfaction to the listener, particularly towards the conclusion of a composition featuring the poetic verses and rhythmic notes: "Sangeeta vadya vinoda tandava jata bahutara veda chodyam."

pa ni ni sa - tha ka ja nu tha - sa ni ni

jam thari tha- sa ma ga m pa; ni ma ga

tha ja nu tha ka - ma ga ma ma pa - SA ni ni

tha jam thari - pa; ma ga - tha ri ki ta thom

The auspicious Shiva is adorned in ashes and serpents. His third eye is slightly opened, and his locks of curly hair bathing in the sacred river Ganga which called "Samvriddhi" the abundant wealth and prosperity, flowing from the heavens to the earth.

I recollect Deeskhitar's kriti on jalalingam (water) "जम्बूपते मां पाहि निजानंदामृत बोधं देहि" in Yamuna kalyani raga.

"Oh Jambupati, protect me and bestow upon me the true knowledge which gives nectar of happiness."

Resting on Lord Shiva's tuft, the crescent moon adorned the Himalayas with a silver aura. Representing the deity of Time through its waxing and waning phases, the Moon aligns with the ever-changing nature of time. As a result, Nataraja is acknowledged as the primary deity of Time, known as "mahaa kaala," with "kaala" signifying time. In his gaze, Shiva's eyes embody the sun, moon, and wisdom.

As Nataraja dances, his earring sways in rhythmic cadence, shining on the radiant cheeks of Goddess Parvati. Nataraja's right ear bears a distinctive earring known as "makara Kundala," where "makara" refers to a crocodile and "Kundala" signifies an ear-knob hanging. This earring, shaped like a golden crocodile, is typically worn by males and is a symbol of Shiva's wealth of knowledge. It represents Shiva as the Supreme Guru, particularly in his form as Dakshinamurti.

On the left earlobe hangs a ear hanging, called taatanka, which is the female jewelry, representing divine feminine beauty signifying the femininity of Shiva's left side and portraying him as both male and female, known as ardhanarishvara. The earring on the right ear signifies Shiva's role as a guru and father, while the one on the left represents his nurturing motherly roles, symbolizing Prakriti. Shiva is father, mother and guru.

A cobra gracefully winding around Shiva's neck, enchanted, witnesses the divine dance of Lord Shiva.

It symbolizes a coiling power, specifically the innate power inherent in all beings, known as Kundalini shakti.

It reminded me of Muthuswamy Dikshitar's kriti in Huseni raga. This is attributed to the Vayu lingam situated at Sri Kalahasti near Tirupati, Andhra Pradesh.

श्री कालहस्तीश श्रीतजनावन समीराकार मां पाहि राजमौले एहि

"O Lord of Sri Kalahasti, You who protect those who take refuge in You, and are the form of Samira (air, one of the five elements), please protect me, oh Rajamauli."

Also the snake is represented as "Sankarabharanam" raga, the ornament of shiva, a coiled raga with beautiful gamakas. The sacred thread yajnopaveetham represents purity.

It was a dance that symbolized the eternal cycle of birth and death, and also creation and dissolution. The gods, entranced by the celestial spectacle, bowed in reverence to the king of the cosmic dance.

The divine jugalbandi continued, and the dance of Shiva, the Nataraja, reached its crescendo.

In the melodic verses of Purandaradasa's song,

चन्द्रचूड! शिवि! शङ्कर! पार्वती रमणने!
निनागे नमो नमो!

"Chandracuda! Shiva! Shankara! Parvati Ramanane!

Ninage namo namo!" The seekers' divine arti is woven strongly.

Garlanded in devotion, Lord Shiva stands, in a raga born from Dheera Shankarabharanam.

The "Abhinaya Darpana" by Nandikeshvara is a comprehensive text on dance, consisting of 4000 verses. In this text, Nandikeshwara beautifully articulates that the entirety of the universe, both movable and immovable, manifests as the physical embodiment of Lord Shiva. He reverently depicts all literature as his divine discourse, while the celestial bodies—the sun, moon, and star symbolize his graceful movements.

I felt a special presence in the ajapa mandapam, as if the whole universe joined in the cosmic celebration.

Muthuswamy Dikshitar adored Lord Thyagaraja and found blissful union with Him through singing in Ananda Bhairavi raga.

"tyāgarāja yoga vaibhavaṁ sadashiivaṁ"

a composition by Muthuswamy Dikshitar demonstrates his musical prowess and command on Sanskrit.

Muthuswamy Dikshitar takes refuge at Lord Tyagaraja (Lord Shiva). He says Lord Tyagaraja is greater than the greatest, and he is smaller than the smallest object. He is beyond human understanding." aNOraNeeyana mahatOmaheeyana".

A noteworthy feature of this piece is the pallavi, which contains a phrase derived from "Tyagaraja Yoga Vaibhavam" to "Vam!" referred to as "Gopucca" (cow's tail) yati, gradually tapering towards the end.

Tyāgarāja yoga vaibhavaṁ sadashiivaṁ

Tyāgarāja yoga vaibhavaṁ sadashrayāmi

Tyāgarāja yoga vaibhavaṁ

Agarāja yoga vaibhavaṁ

Rāja yoga vaibhavaṁ

yoga vaibhavaṁ

Vaibhavaṁ

Bhavaṁ

Vam

त्यागराज योग वैभवं सदाशिवं

त्यागराज योग वैभवं सदाश्रयामि

त्यागराज योग वैभवं

अगराज योग वैभवं

राज योग वैभवं

योग वैभवं

वैभवं

भवं

वं

Additionally, the madhyama kaalam section showcases a phrase, starting from "Sham" and extending to "Siva..Swaroopa Prakaasham" and beyond.

Sham

Prakasham

Swaroopa Prakasam

Tatva Swaroopa Prakasham

Sakala Tatva swaroopa prakasham

Siva saktyaadi sakala tatva swaroopa prakasham

This style of writing is called "Shrotovaaha" yati, denotes a progression that commences on a small scale and gradually expands over time. For example, a river, originating at a place, begins its journey as a modest stream. As it courses through diverse landscapes, the river gathers strength and volume, gradually expanding its waters, transitioning from narrow to wide, finally merges in an ocean.

I realize that his knowledge is transcendental and beyond material existence. The spiritual world takes us to eternal life full of bliss. I bow to Nataraja. His grace is unlimited.

To me, the enchanting performance resembled an Indian classical concert on the stage. The sages were like the audience, rasikas enjoying the music and dance.

"Sangeetha ratnakaram" one of the great old books on Indian music says

गीतं वाद्यं तथा नृत्यं त्रयं सङ्गीतमुच्यते।

"Geetam vadyam tatha nrityam trayam sangeetamuchyate" The term singing (Geetam), playing instruments (Vadyam), and dancing (Nrityam) are collectively known as Sangeetham (music).

CHAPTER 7

SABHA

Long ago, in ancient times in India, the art of dance graced the king's court as "rajaasthanam." During these royal gatherings, a unique dance form emerged, earning the names "kutcheri ata" and "darbar ata."

This distinctive dance wasn't just about graceful movements; it also embraced classical music, earning it the title "Karnataka" or "Carnatic." Dancers adorned the royal courts, weaving tales through their rhythmic steps and melodic expressions.

Led by a skilled dancer, groups of performers would enchant the audience with their synchronized movements and captivating expressions. This dance wasn't just a visual spectacle; it was a form of entertainment that resonated with poets, pandits, scientists, and kings alike.

In the harmonious blend of dance and classical music, these performances became a source of joy, inspiration, and cultural richness for all who gathered in the royal courts. The legacy of "kutcheri ata" and "darbar ata" echoed through time, a celebration of art that transcended boundaries and delighted the hearts of diverse audiences.

Over time, what began as dance concerts accompanied by classical background music evolved into delightful performances of classical vocal and instrumental music, captivating audiences. Picture yourself in South India, where people discuss something known as "Kutcheri," believed to have originated from the royal courts where such performances, known as kutcheri atta, were held. You can listen to Carnatic music at concerts held in auditoriums worldwide, known as kutcheris or sabhas.

In 17th, 18th, and 19th century South India, classical music prospered under the patronage of both kings' courts and temples.

In South India, in places like Tamil Nadu, Karnataka, and Andhra Pradesh, when they say Kutcheri, they mean a concert where they sing and play Carnatic classical music. The word Kutcheri comes from the Urdu language. In Urdu, it means a performance or concert.

Kutcheris are like special concerts in South India where talented musicians show off their outstanding skills in Carnatic music.

Now, these concerts happen in places like auditoriums, temples, or cultural centers. The musicians can sing (that's called vocal music), play instruments, and sometimes even dance.

Nowadays, we watch these Kutcheris on the internet. So, even if we're not in India, we can still enjoy the music from these concerts on your computer or tablet.

Seated gracefully on the floor, South Indian violinists cross their legs, with the right foot extending outward. They skillfully place the scroll of their instrument on the ankle of the right foot, allowing the back of the violin to find its place against the musician's left collarbone or shoulder. This particular playing posture is esteemed as ideal for Indian music, granting the hand the freedom to navigate the fingerboard with ease. Beyond that, it establishes a stable foundation, facilitating the execution of rapid alankar (ornamentations), a hallmark of South Indian musical expression.

The essence of a concert is often shaped by spontaneity and improvisation. A musician's proficiency is demonstrated through their skill. Kutcheris generally adhere to a traditional format and are structured with a sequence of musical items. Indian classical music is performed both vocally and instrumentally.

Tambura is a string instrument that generates "sruti" which is a sound that resonates when it strums, which is used in Indian music concerts. Sruti plays a crucial role in every concert, serving as the fundamental pitch (fixed scale) upon which the entire performance is built. The Tambura has four strings usually, some of them having 5 strings tuned as pa-sa-sa-sa-sa (lower sa). The goal of the tambura player in any concert is to play the tambura uninterrupted adhering to the sruti of the musician. For example, when a musician sings in C sruti for example, all the accompanists in the concert would tune their instruments to C sruti. Tambura does not follow the rhythm of the composition that the musician performs. It follows its own rhythm, enhancing the beauty of the presentation as the musician sings various compositions adhering to sruti.

The concert typically commences with a Varnam, which is like an appetizer during a meal. In Sanskrit, Varnam means color. Varnam derives its name from its purpose of showcasing the color of the raga. It incorporates sahityam (lyrics) elements and musical patterns with notes (swaras) such as muktai swaram and chitta swaram. It is commonly set to rhythmic cycles like Adi talam or ata talam. This initial piece serves as a warm-up for the musician, aiding in establishing the musical scale and setting the mood for the rest of the performance.

Following the Varnam, the musician proceeds to present a series of compositions known as Kritis. These Kritis are songs composed by revered Carnatic maestros such as Tyagaraja, Muthuswami Dikshitar, Syama Sastri, Purandaradasar, and other renowned composers. These compositions are celebrated for their intricate melodies, poetic lyrics, and profound emotional expression.

Typically, these Kritis are presented by initially rendering the raga alapana (melodic framework), followed by neraval, which involves embellished improvisations on a specific line of the composition, and kalpana swaras, where the musician spontaneously presents rhythmic patterns in the form of musical notes.

Throughout the concert, the musician explores various ragas and tala patterns (rhythmic cycles) to showcase their improvisational prowess. A violin solo is played in vocal concerts when the vocal artist finishes performing a raga.

The concert typically concludes with a Mangalam, a composition that offers salutations to the deity, seeking auspiciousness.

Kutcheris hold a position of deep reverence within the culture of South Indian classical music, attracting both connoisseurs and general music enthusiasts. These concerts serve as a vital platform for established musicians as well as emerging talents to showcase their skills and develop a meaningful connection with the audience. The kutcheri tradition carries a profound heritage and remains a thriving and inseparable part of the cultural tapestry of South India.

Kutcheris feature a wide range of musical instruments that play a significant role in the performance. Violin, Mridangam, Kanjira, Tambura, ghatam, morsing are some of the commonly used instruments in a kutcheri. However, some of the concerts can include other instruments such as the Flute, Veena, Nadaswaram, Thavil, etc.

Concert Etiquette

It is said that to truly appreciate music, one should make oneself as silent as possible.

Guidelines for concert etiquette typically adhere to the following principles. Audiences are expected to maintain pin-drop silence while performers are tuning. It is essential to switch off mobile phones during the concert to avoid disruptions. Refrain from getting up or walking out during the performance, as it can be disrespectful and distracting to the artists. Only tap the beat on your lap if you are experienced; otherwise, it may not only look awkward but also distract those around you if you miss the rhythm.

Pay close attention to the rhythmic part of the concert, known as Thani Avarthanam.If the singer doesn't perform a requested song, please refrain from standing and disrupting the concert.

It is generally considered polite to keep your singing low as an audience member at a music concert. The primary focus is usually on the performers, and singing from the audience can be distracting to others. It's important to be mindful of the overall concert experience for everyone attending. If you feel the urge to sing along, try to keep it at a volume that won't disturb those around you.

I think adhering to these guidelines during a music concert enhances our enjoyment of the event.

Ragas like Sankarabharanam are capable of inducing a state of deep calm and semi-trance. To create beautiful music, it is essential to present the right ingredients in the correct proportions. In the rendition of raga alapana, every breath should resonate with raga bhava, and each breath must carry a profound melodic essence.

The legendary musician Dr. Sripada Pinakapani, was a medical doctor, and an exceptional teacher. He mentored numerous renowned vocalists from Andhra Pradesh. Dr. Sripada Pinakapani expressed his admiration, stating that he became a devoted fan of Ariyakudi Ramanuja Iyengar's singing. The beauty of Ariyakudi's kriti renditions, the intricacies of the sangatis in his alapana, his skillful use of gamakas, the delicacy evident in his niraval and swaraprastara, along with the overall compactness of his concerts, left a profound impact on Pinakapani.

The esteemed Sripada Pinakapani once recounted an experience, sharing that when his parents visited Rameswaram in December 1930, he requested to stay in Chennai at his aunt's home. During this time, he immersed himself in a musical feast, savoring performances by Ariyakudi, Flute Swaminatha Pillai, the Karaikudi Brothers, and others. Musiri Subramanya Iyer's niraval for a Tyagaraja kriti in Saraswatimanohari "Enta vedukondu raghava" lingered in his mind for days, and it was from Musiri's music that he learned to sing kritis in vilamba kala (slow tempo) and perform niraval. Niraval or neravu is elaboration of a line of the song using the raga spontaneously.

Pinakapani expressed admiration for Chembai's skill, particularly noting the ease with which Chembai landed on the eduppu of a four-kalai pallavi. Eduppu, a Tamil term, signifies the point at which the music commences within the Tala cycle.

As he was about to leave Madras, his guru Dwaram Venkataswamy Naidu urged him to stay another day, recommending that he listen to an old lady named Dhanammal, a rare and exceptional musician. Intrigued, Pinakapani stayed back and was profoundly moved by Dhanammal's veena performance, considering it a treasure of veena music.

Despite his professional commitments, he dedicated a significant portion of his life to the study and practice of Carnatic Vocal music.

He considered the imparting of knowledge a mission and played a pivotal role in shaping eminent musicians such as Sri Nedunuri Krishnamurti, Voleti Venkateswarulu, Srirangam Gopalaratnam, and my guru Dr. Nookala Chinna Satyanarayana. When I was young, I had the fortunate opportunity of performing a song before Dr. Sripada Pinakapani Garu whom I met through my guruji. After listening to the song, Dr. Sripada Pinakapani Garu blessed me.

Dr. Sripada Pinakapani Garu authored several music books for students, and in his professional capacity his articles were published in international medical journals.

Mudra

All concerts centered on Keerthana in Carnatic music, a song which evolved from Sankeertanam, devotional music. Many classical composers in the Carnatic music tradition, often left a signature or a "mudra" in their compositions. This mudra is essentially a way for the composer to identify themselves within the composition.

- Tyagaraja used "Tyagaraja" in his compositions.
- Muthuswamy Dikshitar used "Guruguha."
- Syama Sastri used "Syama Krishna."
- Papanasan Sivan used "Ramadasa."
- Purandara Dasar used "Purandara Vittala"
- Sadasiva Brahmendra used "Paramahamsa"
- Bhadrachala Ramadas used "Bhadrachala"

Many composers use mudras in a similar fashion. These mudras not only serve as a signature for the composer but also convey their devotion or connection to a specific deity or guru. It's a beautiful tradition that adds depth and personal touch to the compositions. We can observe these while listening to the compositions.

From November to December, Chennai hosts the Margazhi festival, a music season that offers classical artists from around the world an opportunity to showcase their talent. The Carnatic music festival exclusively featuring Carnatic music concerts, harikathas, lecture demonstrations (commonly known as lec-dems), and award/title ceremonies. The title of Sangeetha Kalanidhi, is annually bestowed upon a Carnatic musician by the Madras Music Academy. The title's name is derived from "sangeetha" meaning music, "kala" meaning art, and "nidhi" meaning treasure or ocean.

Organizations come together to help the arts by offering venues and performance opportunities to artists. These are called "sabhas." The prominent sabhas in Chennai include:

Narada Gana Sabha, Sri Krishna Gaana Sabha, Sri Paarthasaarathy Swaami Sabhaa, Sri Thyaaga Brahma Gaana Sabhaa, Indian Fine Arts Society, Madras Music Academy.

Numerous organizations in India serve as venues for Carnatic music concerts. Many sabhas now offer online music concerts as well. You can stay updated by following them on YouTube and other social platforms to enjoy these performances.

Listening to the All India Radio Carnatic music concert is indeed enchanting. I have fond memories of tuning in to these mesmerizing performances from various All India Radio stations like Vijayawada, Hyderabad, Chennai, Bangalore, and Delhi. Each note that fills the airwaves carries the profound legacy of countless maestros who devoted their lives to honing this exquisite art form.

Each musician brings forth their own distinct essence. Some are like mathematicians, others immerse themselves in "bhava," the profound expression of emotion. There are those who reign supreme in melody, captivating audiences as melody queens and melody kings. Some dazzle with their imaginative, creative renditions of raga, kalpana swaras, and neraval, while others enchant with their magical, spellbinding flow of music. Indeed, some musicians possess the remarkable ability to embody all these facets.

Renowned vocalist Dr. Mangalampalli Balamuralikrishna was not only a master vocalist but also proficient in playing the viola, mridangam, and kanjira instruments. Similarly, my mentor, Dr. Nookala Chinna Satyanarayana, was a violin virtuoso in addition to his vocal prowess. Flutist Mali showcased brilliance on the violin as well. TV Gopalakrishna excels in both Carnatic and Hindustani music, showcasing his talent on the mridangam. Violinist MS Gopalakrishnan was adept in both Carnatic and Hindustani styles. Vocalist TN Seshagopalan, besides his vocal mastery, is also proficient in playing the veena and harmonium, and is recognized as an exponent of harikatha. The list goes on, showcasing the multifaceted talents of numerous musicians who excel not only as vocalists but also demonstrate exceptional skill in playing various instruments.

The audience sits rapt, their attention captivated by the maestros who, with each passing minute, redefine ragas, meditating on indescribable "Om," weaving intricate melodies that creates nectar of happiness for the thirsty soul.

In earlier times, the veena served as the accompanying instrument in music concerts, until the violin emerged as a better choice for accompaniment over the past 200 years.

CHAPTER 8

SARASWATI VEENA

$\mathcal{V}$eena is a popular, ancient string instrument in India. The national musical instrument of India is called the Saraswati veena! Not many people know about it. The southern region of India uses the "Saraswati veena", and the northern region uses the veena called "Rudra veena".

A plucked string instrument with a rich and resonant sound, the Veena is one of the oldest instruments in South Indian classical music, which mimics the vocals. The Yajur Veda mentions the Veena accompanying the vocal recitations during sacrifices. The Rudra Veena is strongly associated with Lord Shiva, who created it. It is said that even the demon king Ravana was a proficient player of the Rudra Veena, and being a devotee of Lord Shiva, Ravana used it to please Lord Shiva.

The tale narrates an incident where Ravana, deeply engrossed in playing the Rudra Veena to delight Lord Shiva, accidentally broke one of its strings. Not wanting to disturb Shiva's enjoyment, Ravana replaced the broken string with one of his nerves. This act showcased Ravana's reverence for Shiva and his dedication to creating joy and contentment for the deity. It stands as a testament to Ravana's deep respect for Lord Shiva and his commitment to honoring the divine through his music using the Veena. There are legendary tales of Sage Agastya engaging in a Veena competition with Ravana, judged by Maha Meru.

Naarada and Tumbura are great devotees of lord Vishnu. Naarada's Veena is renowned as the Mahathi.

On the other hand, Tumbura's Veena is referred to as the Kalavathi.

Long ago, in our ancient tales, it is said that the musical saint Narada originated the idea of Veena. Furthermore, music is associated with Goddess Saraswati, who is considered the deity of this art form. We have imagined the goddess Saraswati playing heavenly music in our minds. This was depicted in a really cool painting by a famous artist, Ravi Varma, revealing exactly how one perceives Saraswati Devi. It's a depiction of her playing beautiful music!

When you hear the music of the veena pioneers, you experience a beautiful blend of aesthetics and intellect. The impressive plucking and fingering techniques create a remarkably rich tone with unimaginable speed. A Veena player is called a "Vainika."

Veena Venkataramana Das was the doyen of Veena and lived in "Veenavari Street" in Vijayanagaram, Andhra Pradesh, India. He had a veena made of sampangi wood. Tanjore Veena is made of jackwood from a jackfruit tree. Mysore Veena is made of blackwood. He can play Veena at six degrees of speed. Once, during a performance at the Senate House in Madras, Venkataramana Das faced an unexpected challenge. Rain began pouring down, creating quite a racket. To minimize the noise, the event organizers tried closing doors and windows. However, Venkataramana Das was undeterred. He boldly declared that he could still make himself heard and insisted that the doors and windows remain open.

The enthralled audience enjoyed the rain songs coming out of Veena.

Beneath the silver Veena's spell, ragas danced in the air,

A melody woven with grace, a musical affair.

As raindrops joined the tune, a celestial blend,

Enthralled hearts listened, a blissful transcend.

Nature's symphony played, raindrops like a gentle choir,

Veena's strings echoed, setting the souls afire.

The downpour and the music, a harmonious embrace,

Captivated hearts swayed, lost in the rhythmic grace.

Sangameswara Sastry, a skilled veena player, was born in 1873 near Bobbili, Vizianagaram. He performed in many places across India and held the "Sangeetha Vidwan" title of Pithapuram Samsthanam. His veena skills even caught the attention of the great poet Rabindranath Tagore, who admired him and invited him to Kolkata. Sangameswara Sastry could make his Veena sound like thunder (Megha garjan) or music bird cuckoo (kokila).

"Veena vadana tattwagnah, shruti jati visarada,

Talajnascha prayasena, Moksha margam sagachhati."

Meaning:

"One who understands the essence of playing the Veena with the knowledge of sruti, laya, walks the path of moksha (salvation)."

On the day Sangameswara Sastry knew his time to leave the earthly body was near, he sensed he had only a few hours left. Lying on his bed, he placed the Veena on his chest and played the "Ananda Bhairavi" raga cheerfully until the very end. As his soul departed, the sweet strains of his veena music accompanied his journey beyond.

Another great vainika vidwan, Veena Doraiswamy Iyenger, is a masterful player of the Veena in contemporary Indian history. He engaged in numerous Jugalbandis, collaborating with renowned Hindustani classical instrumentalists, including Ustad Ali Akbar Khan.

His life was all about music, music, and more music.

In the poignant moments of 1997, Doraiswamy Iyengar made a heartfelt request after enduring weeks of illness. Weak and confined to his bed, he asked for a portrait of Lord Rama to be brought to him. His wife, standing by, tenderly held before his fading eyes a small frame featuring the music trinity—Tyagaraja, Dikshitar, and Syama Sastri. He departed with a whispered prayer of "Janardana," leaving a profound silence behind. His music is eternal and he touched millions with his humility.

The Veena is made up of a big bowl called "Kai" or "Kudam," and it has 24 frets, like metallic rods. You can create ten different kinds of musical embellishments, called gamakas, on it. The first string is called "Sarani," and it's made of steel. The second string is called "Panchamam," and the third and fourth strings are named "Mandram" and "Anumandram," respectively.

Imagine an incredible veena player from Mysore who got an award called "Savyasachi." What's so cool about him? Well, he could play the Veena in both positions. That means he could pluck the strings with his right hand and play them with his left hand, and then switch it up and do it the other way around! It's like being a great vainika with the ability to play the Veena in two different ways!

The sound made by Veena Sambayya from Mysore was so powerful that it was like listening to a hundred Veenas playing together simultaneously. It's like one person making as much music as a whole big group of vainikas! That's pretty amazing.

Chitti Babu was one of the most famous Veena artists of India. Known as "Veena" Chitti Babu, he stood out as an extraordinary Veena maestro. Chitti Babu created a unique style evolving from the principles of Emani "Bani" (tradition/style) of his Guru. His music captivated both connoisseurs and young listeners alike, making his concerts immensely popular and drawing large crowds. On his Veena, he showcased a wide range of styles, from the grandeur of Vedic hymns to the subtlety of a cuckoo's voice, and even ventured into creating his own compositions inspired by Western music. His lovely "Wedding Bells" album is available online for listening.

Chitti Babu famously remarked, "To me, music starts with the letter ‹M,' representing ‹Melody.' Remove that ‹M,' and you're left with ‹USIC' (YOU SICK!)" emphasizing the vital role of melody in music.

CHAPTER 9

GANDHARVA GAANAM

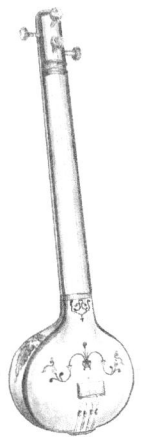

*I*ndian music sparkles like a magnificent gem in the rich tapestry of Indian tradition.

The Kailash Range, highly revered by Hindus, is believed to be around 30 million years old. It took shape during the early phases of the formation of the mighty Himalayan mountains. The sacred mountain and the holy lake, Mansarovar, is in Tibet, with routes from Uttarakhand connecting it to India.

Kailash Mansarovar is the sacred abode of Lord Shiva and Goddess Parvati. It is also said to be inhabited by various divine beings, including Devtas (celestial beings), Ganas (attendants of Shiva), Yakshas (nature spirits), Yogis (spiritual practitioners), Siddha Purushas (enlightened beings), and Gandharvas (celestial musicians). The mystical ambience of Kailash Mansarovar is thought to be a gathering place for these divine entities, making it a spiritually significant and revered location in Hindu mythology.

Indian classical music is often called "Gandharva Vidya," which draws its inspiration from the music of the celestial beings known as Gandharvas. The term "Gandharva Vidya" signifies the profound connection between Indian classical music and the divine musical tradition of the Gandharvas.

Gandharvas are celestial beings in Indian mythology who are closely associated with music and are considered divine musicians. They are known for their captivating voices with extraordinary musical abilities.

Lord Krishna states in the Bhagavad Gita 10.26

"Amongst the Gandharvas I am Chitrarath"

Lord Krishna manifests as Chitraratha among the Gandharvas.

In the Mahabharat epic, the Pandavas found themselves in a forest after escaping from a palace made of lac (laksagriha). There, they encountered and defeated two demons named Hidimba and Baka. One night, while walking along the river Ganga, they heard someone at the river. Arjuna, being curious, went to check and found Citraratha, a powerful Gandharva, enjoying a bath with his wife, Kumbhinasi.

Now, nighttime is reserved for the Gandharvas, and humans weren't supposed to peep in. Chitraratha felt it was impolite of Arjuna to be walking around and peeping into the privacy of the Gandharvas. This led to a fight between Chitraratha and Arjuna. After a tough battle, Arjuna defeated Chitraratha, tied him up, and brought him before his brothers.

Kumbhinasi, seeing her husband defeated, approached Dharmaraja (Yudhistira) and pleaded for his release. Dharmaputra, being wise, advised Arjuna to set Chitraratha free. Upon his release, Citraratha taught Arjuna a powerful skill called Chaksusividya, a magical art that allowed one to see anything and everything in the three worlds – Heaven, Earth, and the netherworld – with the naked eyes. Chitraratha gave chariots and hundreds of horses to Pandavas.

Gandharvas, revered in ancient lore, are celestial beings known for their enchanting singing abilities. The art of music itself is referred to as "Gandharva Vidya," a sacred gift bestowed upon humanity by the Gandharvas. Inhabiting the celestial realm known as Gandharva planet, its inhabitants possess melodious voices and a deep affinity for singing.

In another captivating tale, a childless Gandharva approached the sage Vasista, seeking guidance on how to have a child. Moved by his plight, Vasista advised the Gandharva to chant the sacred Shiva Panchakshari mantra. Following the sage's instructions, the Gandharva fervently prayed to Lord Shiva, who was pleased by his devotion, granted him a son. Named "Upabrahma" by Guru Vasista, the child was none other than the illustrious Narada.

Epic sagas like the Mahabharata often depict extraordinary beings such as the Gandharvas. Renowned for their musical and dance prowess, they are believed to reside in the vicinity of Mount Kailash, adding to the mystique surrounding their existence.

Gandharva Vidya encapsulates the essence of Indian classical music, representing its divine origins, spiritual depth, and the timeless beauty of this cherished art form.

Naarada and Tumbura

India, known as "Bharata Varsha," is revered as the land that has given birth to numerous sages and selfless, pious individuals. The rituals established by these ancient sages continue to be practiced even today. Among these illustrious figures is Narada Maharshi, a revered Sangeetha Maharshi, who passionately adhered to Vedic dharma and became an esteemed exponent of music.

Narada, the revered sage, served as the guru to prominent figures such as Vyasa, Valmiki, Prahlada, and Dhruv.

Legend has it that during Lord Vishnu's Vamana incarnation, he covered the entire land with one foot and extended his second foot to occupy the sky. At that moment, Brahma, desiring to offer a welcome and perform worship, sought to cleanse Lord Vishnu's feet with water. Brahma created Narada for this purpose, and thus, the name "Narada" in Sanskrit signifies the one who fetches water. Upon his birth, Narada sought the guidance of the deity Saraswati and learned the art of music from her. Later, he visited Vayu Loka and received the divine musical instrument Veena, known as "Mahathi."

Tumbura, an accomplished Gandharva known for his devotional singing, gained immense fame. However, Narada, consumed by jealousy, lost his peace of mind. Seeking resolution, Narada approached Lord Vishnu and requested guidance on furthering his musical prowess. Vishnu directed Narada to the Manasottara Mountain to learn from Jnana Bandhu, an owl renowned for his musical skills. Although Narada received training from Jnana Bandhu, he couldn't surpass the exceptional musician Tumbura.

Once upon a time, Narada and Tumburu wanted to sing in praise of the Lord. Both were so good that the Lord couldn't decide whose singing pleased Him more. To find a solution, the Lord called upon Hanuman, known for being an expert in poetry, drama, music, dance, and all things artistic.

So, Hanuman arrived, and a musical contest began. Tumburu played his veena, Kalavathi, and the whole universe stood still in awe of his enchanting music. Even Hanuman nodded in appreciation. Then came Narada's turn, playing his veena, Mahathi, and his celestial music melted everything that was frozen before. Both were outstanding, and everyone eagerly awaited Hanuman's judgment.

Instead of announcing a winner, Hanuman asked for their veenas and removed the frets (the vertical strips on which the strings run). He handed the fretless veenas back to them and told them to play. Confused, they asked how the veena could be played without the frets. Hanuman silently took the fretless veena, used a small bamboo stick, and played expertly.

He sang and played, captivating all the divine beings. When they looked around after a while, they saw Lord Sri Hari Himself among them, listening attentively to Hanuman's music. Narada and Tumburu bowed down, acknowledging that Hanuman wasn't just the greatest devotee but also the most accomplished musician. His devotion and musical skill had won the heart of the Lord Hari Himself.

Narada then returned to Vishnu and implored him to teach music directly. Vishnu assured Narada that in his next incarnation as Krishna, he would impart musical knowledge. During Krishna's avatar, Narada was sent to learn music from Jambavati, but even then, he struggled to achieve perfection.

Finally, Lord Krishna personally instructed Narada, transforming him into a realized musician.

Narada attained musical perfection and became a genius in his own right.

While Narada is often mistakenly labeled as a troublemaker or lover of quarrels (Kalahari Priya), he is actually a revered sage who possesses profound knowledge of the universe. He brings auspiciousness and aids others in achieving self-realization. Pleased with Dhruva's devotion, Narada taught him the sacred mantra "Om Namo Narayanaya." Dhruva followed Narada's guidance and became the Dhruva Nakshatra, the shining pole star in the sky. In Hindu marriage rituals, the groom is often shown the Dhruva Nakshatra on the wedding night, symbolizing the unwavering devotion of child Dhruva to Lord Vishnu. Narada's influence ensures such impactful conclusions in the lives he encounters.

Narada authored numerous Puranas and the Bhakti Sutras, which were followed by saints and devotees alike. The renowned Carnatic composer Tyagaraja Swamy was an ardent follower of Narada's Bhakti Sutras. It is believed that Narada appeared to Tyagaraja Swamy and presented him with a book called Swararnava, containing the secrets of ragas and music.

Sadasiva Brahmendra, who lived in the 15th and 16th centuries, was a revered saint, composer of Carnatic music, and an Advaita philosopher. He is often referred to as a "Siddha Purusha," which signifies a realized and enlightened being.

He renounced worldly life and underwent rigorous spiritual practice for eighteen years. His guru taunted him for being talkative, prompting him to take a vow of silence that he maintained for the rest of his life. He lived as a wandering naked (avadhUta) sannyasi, and the songs he composed remain highly popular. Some of his songs "Manasa Sancharare," "Pibare Rama Rasam," "Smaravaram," "Bhajare Raghuveeram," "Bruhi Mukundeti," "Bhajare Gopalam".

Sadasiva Brahmendra's compositions in Carnatic music have left a lasting impact. He authored several books, one of which includes a commentary on the Yoga Sutras of Patanjali. During his lifetime, Sadasiva Brahmendra is believed to have manifested numerous miracles, with some of the most notable instances outlined below.

On the banks of the Cauvery River in Mahadhanapuram, children requested him to take them to Madurai, over 100 miles away, for an annual festival. The saint instructed them to close their eyes, and upon reopening them seconds later, they discovered themselves in Madurai.

During another instance, as he meditated on the banks of the Cauvery river, a sudden flood carried him away, witnessed by the villagers. Several weeks later, while some villagers were digging near a mound of earth, their shovels struck his body. To everyone's amazement, he woke up and walked away.

The book "Autobiography of a Yogi" by Paramahamsa Yogananda briefly notes the location of his jeeva samadhi site. Sadasiva Brahmendra attained Jeeva Samadhi in Nerur, Tamil Nadu.

Venkatesa Ayyaval, his old-time classmate, was the one who broke his silence, perhaps once or twice. In the days of his discipleship, Sadasiva Brahmendra used to sing melodious bhajans.

Vocal Singing goes beyond regular human abilities and, with a pure mind, becomes an instrument of divine purpose.

Vocal music is considered the highest and most prominent form of expression in the Carnatic music tradition of South India. Vocals are revered as the origin of all instruments. Throughout history, instruments have strived to imitate the beauty and expressiveness of the human voice. Vocal music is considered divine and indeed bestowed upon us as a gift.

It involves the melodic rendition of compositions, improvisation, and the exploration of various ragas (melodic scales) and talas (rhythmic cycles).

Now, when they perform vocal music, they sing beautiful songs, make up music on the spot (that's called improvisation), and play around with different melodies (called ragas) and rhythms (they call them talas). It's like a musical journey exploring all these cool sounds and making the music sound amazing!

In the Bhagavad Gita, verse 10.22, it is stated:

"Vedaanam samavedosmi"

This translates to:

"I am the Samaveda amongst the Vedas."

Among the four Vedas—the Ṛig Veda, Yajur Veda, Sama Veda, and Atharva Veda—the Sama Veda holds a special place. It specifically highlights the divine glories and attributes of God. The Sama Veda is known for its melodic nature and is sung in reverence to the Supreme Lord.

Indian music traces its origins to Samaveda, which evolved from precise intonations used in religious chants.

In devotional chanting, one engages and sings to God deeply and affectionately. The South Indian classical music is evolved from the vedas. The sama ganam is rendered using vocals. Vocal expression is spontaneous. This is why Vocal music is highly regarded as a cherished gift in India.

Vocal music holds a distinct advantage over other forms as it combines the power of melody with the expressive capacity of words. One can directly praise the divine or eloquently convey a wide range of human sentiments and emotions through vocal music. It is a powerful medium to connect with both the spiritual and emotional realms.

The vocalists, often accompanied by instruments, use their voice to convey the beauty and intricacy of the musical elements. The vocalist's voice becomes the primary instrument through which they bring out the nuances of the compositions and engage in improvisations.

Chembai Vaidyanatha Bhagavather, a renowned musician, excels in swara kalpana (swara singing), a unique feature of Carnatic music. His resonant voice effortlessly captivates large audiences, reaching even higher pitches flawlessly. His noble voice makes him a favorite among the masses. The great singer K. J. Yesudas took advanced music training from Chembai Vaidyanatha Bhagavathar. K. J. Yesudas is widely admired for his exceptional voice, which has indeed touched the hearts of millions and left a lasting impression through his singing. In 2003, a billionaire and businessman presented Yesudas with his Rolls-Royce Silver Spirit as a gift following a concert in Dubai.

Dr. Mangalampalli Balamurali Krishna, a renowned Indian classical vocalist in the Carnatic style, gave mesmerizing concerts worldwide. He was a vocalist and skilled in playing instruments. He had great skills in singing Rabindra Sangeet in the Bengali language. He received the rare Chevalier award from the French government for his significant contribution to enriching French cultural heritage.

M. S. Subbulakshmi, a popular Indian classical vocalist, was the first musician to be awarded the "Bharat Ratna" (the highest civilian award in India). She received rare appreciation from Helen Keller, a famous American author who was deaf and blind. Keller described Subbulakshmi's music as beautiful. Subbulakshmi's performances reached millions of fans across the world, and she brought Carnatic music to the West through her appearances at the Edinburgh Festival and the United Nations. M. S. Subbulakshmi's renditions of "Sri Venkateswara Suprabhatam," "Annamacharya Keertanas," and "Bhaja Govindam," "Bhavayami" are cherished by music enthusiasts and rasikas. Her soulful and impeccable singing brings out the spiritual essence of these compositions. Listening to these pieces allows one to experience the depth of her musical prowess and the profound spirituality embedded in the classical renditions. It's a wonderful recommendation for anyone who appreciates the beauty of Indian classical music and devotional compositions.

On the midnight of August 15, 1947, the song "Aaduvome" by Subramanya Bharati sung by my guru D. K. Pattammal was broadcast by All India Radio to mark India's independence, stirring the patriotic hearts of millions of Indians. D. K. Pattammal's Tamil melodies, including "Sivakama Sundari" and "Yaro Ivar Yaro, Eppadi Padinaro," are deeply etched in memory. The compositions are filled with essence raga and expressions.

We can enjoy online concerts by various vocal artists like M. S. Subbulakshmi, D. K. Pattammal, M. L. Vasanthakumari, Srirangam Gopalaratnam, Dr. Mangalampalli Balamurali Krishna, T. M. Krishna, Nedunuri Krishnamurthy, K. V. Narayanaswamy, M. D Ramanathan, Voleti Venkateswarlu, GNB, Semmangudi Srinivasa Iyer, Ariyakudi Ramanuja Iyengar, D. K. Jayaraman, Maharajapuram Santhanam, Madurai Mani Iyer, Chembai Vaidyanath Bhagavatar, K. J. Yesudas, Sudha Raghunathan, Sowmya, Unnikrishnan, Alathur brothers, Trichur brothers, Bombay Jayashree, Priya sisters.

Furthermore, my guruji, "Mahamahopadhyaya" Dr. Nookala Chinna Satyanarayana, had designed an extensive collection of online listen-and-learn music series. These resources provide a valuable opportunity for individuals to learn music online, enhancing their musical knowledge and skills of Carnatic music.

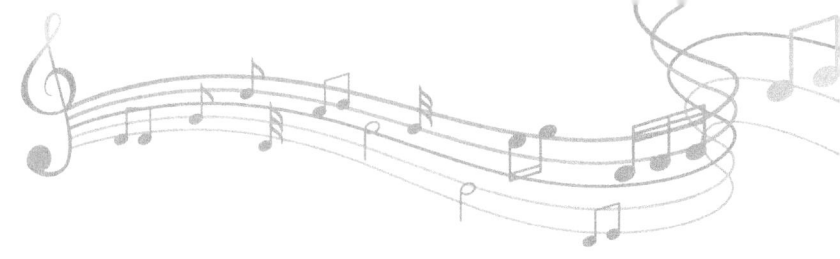

CHAPTER 10

FIDELU

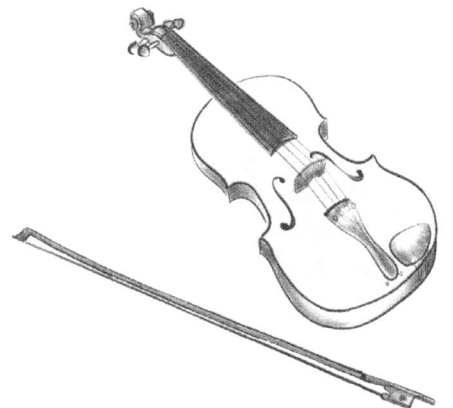

$\mathcal{T}$he violin, to me, is an instrument of emotion. Its melodies express deepest joy stirring the depths of the soul. The Violin serves as an accompanying instrument in South Indian music concerts, and it can also be featured in solo violin concerts.

Once, Pythagoras, a Greek philosopher born around 500 B.C., a man of excellent knowledge, walked past a blacksmith's shop and heard the hammers striking the anvil. He noticed that some hits made higher sounds than others. Curious, he went into the shop and saw they used hammers of different sizes. Some were big, others small, but they were related by ratios like one being twice the size of another. Pythagoras thought these ratios explained the different pitches.

Pythagoras found out that if you have a string and cut it to be exactly half the length of another string, the sound it makes when you hit or pluck it will be exactly one octave higher. If you cut a string in half, its sound will be one octave higher, and the string vibrates twice as fast. If you divide it by three, the tone will be an octave and a bit higher, and the string will vibrate three times as fast. So, the length and the pitch are connected in a unique way.

It is a historical reality that Pythagoras drew inspiration from Indian music knowledge and incorporated it into the Western musical system.

Captain Day, a seasoned Western musician, acknowledged and affirmed this influence in his book "The Musical Instruments of South India," highlighting that instruments such as the Violin, Flute, Piano, and

Guitar originated in India. He mentioned that the piano's origins can be traced back to the Aryans.

The Violin, considered the most popular string instrument worldwide, is thought to have originated in India. After journeying to the Western music world, it returned to its homeland and became prominent in South Indian concerts about 150 years ago. Muthuswamy Dikshitar suggested it as the ideal accompanying instrument during that period.

Around 5000 B.C., Ravana invented a string instrument known as "Ravana Hastam," also called Ravanahatha or Ravanastram.

It is an age-old bowed instrument, played with a bow, discovered in Sri Lanka. The resonating chamber of the Ravanahatha was made from a gourd, a halved coconut shell, or a hollowed-out cylinder of wood. The instrument was referenced in the "Panditaradhya Charitra" within the depiction of the Srisaila Mountains by poet Palkuri Somanathudu. The same book noted that the Ravana Veena is different from the Ravana Hasta.

Before the invention of the Ravana hasta, there existed a string instrument called "Pinaki," which was played by Lord Shiva. The "Penna" instrument played in Assam and Manipur was considered by a British writer as "Pinaki." In the thirteenth century,

Sarjna Deva's book "Sangeetha Ratnakaram" made reference to the instrument called "Pinaki." Over time, an instrument named "Rabab" emerged, named after "Ravani." The ancient book "Sangeetha Makarandam" makes reference to "Ravani."

The "Rabab" instrument inspired the Persians, who brought it to Persia. Subsequently, it made its way to Spain with the name "Rabel" and later to France, where French musicians played it as the "Rabec." Eventually, the instrument became known in Europe as the "Violin" Around 1684, it evolved into the Viola. However, credit for the modern Violin's design is often given to the Italian luthiers of the 16th century, with Andrea Amati and his descendants, particularly Antonio Stradivari, as influential figures in its refinement and popularization. The Violin, as we know it today, evolved through the craftsmanship of various luthiers in the violin-making center of Cremona, Italy.

The Violin, the queen of musical instruments, finally arrived in its homeland in the 18th century. It made its way to Tiruvarur and sought the blessings of the esteemed musician and composer Tyagaraja Swamy. Balasamy Dikshitar, a member of Muthuswamy Dikshitar's family (1786–1858), embraced the instrument with passion and made it popular.

Ponnu Swamy, Govindaswamy Pillai, Tumarada Sangameshwara Sastry, Dwaram Venkata Swamy Naidu, M. S. Gopalakrishnan, Kunnakkudi Vaidyanathan, Lalgudi G Jayaraman, L. Subramaniam, T. N. Krshnan, Ganesh - Kumaresh were some of the legends in Violin.

The first half of 2013 witnessed the loss of two legends M. S. Gopalakrishnan and Lalgudi G. Jayaraman.

The legendary violinist Lalgudi Jayaraman inspired millions of music seekers. He was an incredible music composer. He lived and breathed music.

A remarkable story unfolded in Muscat during one of Lalgudi sir's violin concerts. Someone in the audience shared this tale that showed how powerful music can be. In 2009, a music enthusiast, deeply moved by Lalgudi sir's beautiful performance of "Mohana Rama" song in Mohana raga, Tyagaraja Swamy kriti, on the Violin, decided to give up all her worldly connections. She chose a spiritual path, retiring to an ashram on the outskirts of Chennai.

This story highlights the strong impact of his music. It's not just about enjoying the music; it touched the listener's heart so profoundly that it led her to a journey of spiritual reflection and retreat.

M.S. Gopala Krishnan, popularly known as M.S.G., was synonymous with Violin. He was incredible. His violin expressions are simply remarkable. He was a teacher to great music directors like Ilayaraja. He was amazing with the Violin, playing it perfectly, using the bow skillfully, and creating beautiful melodies for 75 years, a rare feat for any musician. The famous violinist Yehudi Menuhin once said, "I have never heard such a violin in all my travels." When he played ragas, it brought a sense of divine joy. His popular tunes included Nalinakanti, Pantuvarali, Hameer Kalyani, Sindhubhairavi, Kumudakriya, and the song Bhavanuta in Mohanam. I am a fan of his wonderful music.

M.S.G. always said – "Like food, like breath, like a violin." He led a humble life, offering performances without charge for many sabhas and never seeking anything in return. M.S.G.'s enchanting music, embracing both Carnatic and Hindustani styles, will permanently reside in our hearts.

Another legend, Tirukkodikaval Krishna Iyer (1857–1913), holds a respected position among the experts in violin playing. He was a prominent violin artist in his era and belonged to the Shishya parampara (discipleship tradition) of Muthuswami Dikshitar. He was skilled in five languages: Sanskrit, Marathi, Tamil, Telugu, and Kannada. He honed his skills by playing 4, 8, 16, 32, and 64 notes in a single stroke of the bow, achieving a high speed in violin playing. During the Dasara festival series in Kakinada, Andhra Pradesh, he delivered a solo performance on the Violin. On that occasion, he played alapana and Pallavi in the Saveri raga for over four hours. The audience lost track of time as his violin performance was exceptionally captivating. He played a crucial role in elevating the status of the Violin as a suitable instrument for Carnatic music. Since then, no classical music concert in South India has been deemed complete without including the Violin.

Dwaram Venkata Swamy Naidu, renowned for his mastery of the violin, embraced the English bowing technique, offering a distinctiveness to his rendition of taanam, rhythmic movement of notes. His bold interpretation of ragas captivated even those unfamiliar with classical music. Through the incorporation of quarter tones, he skillfully expressed the true picture of a raga, evoking quintessential emotions of each raga. For instance, his rendition of "Swara Raaga Sudha" in the Sankarabharanam raga is truly delightful to the ears. We can easily find this masterpiece online to enjoy its beauty.

Thinking back to a special memory from three decades ago, I remember a remarkable moment spent with the renowned violinist Dwaram Mangatayaru, who was the daughter of the legendary Dwaram Venkata

Swamy Naidu. During the time I was pursuing my degree, she visited my guruji's house and graciously demonstrated the intricacies of the Shankarabharam raga. Her mastery of the great Dwaram violin techniques was evident, leaving a lasting impression on me. The performance of "Sankarabharanam" by both the great violinists was a moment of pure musical magic that I will always treasure. I have a feeling that the downpour of the nectar of the raga indeed takes us to the infinite bliss.

CHAPTER 11

BEATS AND HEART BEATS

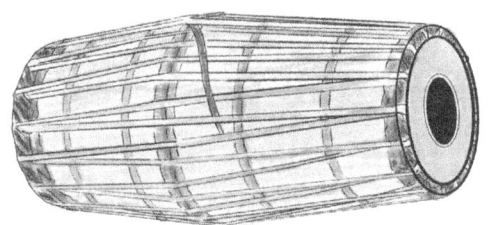

The Tyagarajaswamy temple is renowned for a unique percussion instrument known as "panchamukavadhya" or "Kudamuzha". "Pancha mukha" refers to its five faces, and "vadya" denotes instrument. Through generations, this musical treasure has remained under the care of a single-family, enduring the test of time. Legend has it that Nandi, the divine bull, played this instrument during Lord Shiva's cosmic dance, the Tandavam.

Nandi (Nandikeshwara), the sacred bull, is Lord Shiva's devoted vehicle and represents being attentive and showing interest, care, and love towards others. In many Hindu temples, a statue of Nandi is placed facing the main deity, signifying his eternal dedication.

When Nandi was five, he became proficient in the Vedas and sacred scriptures. Nandikeshwara became a Guru after acquiring divine knowledge from Shiva (consciousness) and Parvati (energy). Nandi, the bull, is the player of the Mridangam, a percussion instrument that creates a sound that helps us find the god's realization.

In a story from the Vishnu Purana, when the gods (Devas) and demons (Asuras) were stirring the ocean of milk to get divine nectar, a dangerous poison (halahala) came out. Everyone got scared, but Lord Shiva drank the poison and retained it in his throat, resulting in his throat turning blue. That's why he's called Neelakantha, meaning the one with a blue throat.

Some poison spilled, and Nandikeeswara, Shiva's follower, quickly consumed it. Despite the chaos, Nandikeeswara, through his meditative practices, stayed focused on the present. He managed his emotions well, helping clean up the spilled poison without getting overwhelmed.

Rhythm is the heartbeat of the song. Without rhythm, there is no entertainment guaranteed. Renowned composers in South India have created many beautiful songs: Tyagaraja, Muthuswamy Dikshitar, and Syama Sastri. Other composers also craft songs in different musical scales called ragas. Songs are a beautiful blend of lyrics and music, offering a swift and expressive form of artistic expression.

The speed of our heartbeat is connected to the rhythm of a song. When we hear a fast-paced rock or movie song, it indicates that the music band or movie team is feeling excited or anxious, as their heartbeat seems to match the quick beat of the music.

When you listen to Indian classical music compositions, you'll notice that they have a slower pace when compared to super fast-beat songs. This is because the composer's blood pressure tends to be normal, unlike someone experiencing a roller coaster of emotions. Listening to classical music, especially a raga like Ananda Bhairavi, can help maintain your normal blood pressure.

Likewise, the rhythmic beats of Indian percussion instruments like Mridangam, ghatam, kanjira, and thavil bring comfort and support to soulful compositions. The authentic beats of the Mridangam create a rhythmic experience that can make you forget yourself in the joy and bliss of "chidanandam," the highest level of happiness.

Mridangam is a double-headed drum, the primary percussion instrument in Carnatic music. The Mridangam finds its roots in Indian mythology, where it is believed that Lord Nandi, the Bull God who was the escort of Lord Shiva, possessed exceptional skill as a percussionist. Lord Nandi would play the Mridangam during the majestic performance of the "Thandavam" dance by Lord Shiva. This mythological connection highlights the ancient and revered lineage of the Mridangam in Indian musical traditions.

Tyagaraja Swamy, in his composition

"Sogasuga mridanga talamu" in Sri ranjani ragam,

Extols the elegance and grace of the Mridangam, recognizing its significance in pleasing the divine. He reflects on the immense skill and courage required to masterfully play the Mridangam, suggesting that only a truly valorous individual can do justice to this instrument in order to please the divine.

The term "tala" comes from the Sanskrit root "tal," which means to strike with the palm. Musicians maintain the rhythm by waving their hands through clapping. Mridangam leads to talam, which refers to the rhythmic framework or time measure in which compositions are performed. The system of talams is diverse and complex, with various rhythmic patterns and cycles. Each talam has a specific structure, which includes the number of beats in a cycle, the arrangement of laghus and dhrutams (subdivisions of beats), and the hand gestures used to keep time. The talam system provides a framework for rhythmic improvisation and composition in Carnatic music. The composition can be set to any of the seven talas Dhruva tala, Mathya tala, Jumpe tala, Ata tala, Eka tala, Rupaka tala, Triputa tala or Adi tala which belongs to Triputa tala.

In the past, Mridangam, a percussion instrument, did not have notations to guide its playing. The knowledge and techniques of playing the Mridangam were traditionally passed down from guru to disciple through oral transmission.

However, in recent times, notations for Mridangam have emerged. These notations provide a written system to represent the rhythmic patterns and compositions played on the Mridangam. They serve as a valuable tool for learning and practicing the instrument, allowing students to study and understand the compositions more comprehensively.

While the traditional method of learning from a guru remains integral, the inclusion of notations has provided an additional resource for mridangam students to enhance their understanding and mastery of the instrument.

The realm of Mridangam playing has witnessed the brilliance of maestros like Palghat Mani Iyer, Karaikudi Mani, T. K. Murthy, Umayalpuram K. Sivaraman, Thiruvarur Bakthavathsalam, and Yella Venkateswara Rao. These esteemed artists have attained mastery over the Mridangam, demonstrating unparalleled skill and artistry in their performances. Their contributions have shaped the landscape of percussion in Carnatic music and continue to inspire generations of aspiring musicians.

Ghatam: The ghatam is a percussion instrument which is a clay pot with a narrow mouth. By varying the pitch and tone using different hand techniques, it creates a unique rhythmic texture in kutcheris. The recognition of the ghatam as a significant instrument in the Carnatic music system is relatively recent, spanning the last 100 to 150 years. During this time, it has gained esteemed status in the realm of serious musical performances. Notably, Vikku Vinayakram stands as one of the illustrious artists who has made invaluable contributions to the art of playing the ghatam. His mastery and talent have further elevated the instrument's prominence in the musical landscape.

Kanjira is also a percussion instrument widely used in Carnatic music concerts and it is a good supporting instrument for Mridangam.

CHAPTER 12

HARIDASU

Uncha Vritti

The other day, I visited the great music composer, Tyagaraja Swamy's house. Inside, it felt so peaceful, as if the air itself was singing in Todi raga. The walls seemed to be in meditation, chanting "Rama," revealing Tyagaraja Swamy's deep devotion to Lord Rama. In my mind, I pictured the maestro lost in his music, his disciples writing notations for his compositions, crafting tunes that would stay with us for generations. It was a special moment, feeling the connection between the walls and the melodies—a timeless echo of devotion.

Tyagaraja swamy lived in thirumanjana veedhi (street) in thiruvaiyaru. In the early morning, he would go to the nearby Kaveri river with his disciples to take a holy dip and bathe in its waters. Tyagaraja Swamy practiced the renunciation of worldly pleasures and lived for the god.

I remember Saint Tyagaraja's song "Haridasulu vedale mucchatagani. Anandamaye dayalo," set to the enchanting Yamuna Kalyani raga, capturing the profound serenity of Krishna bhakti on the banks of the Yamuna.

A beautiful scene unfolds as Haridas, the devotional singers, grace us with their enchanting presence. Watching them sing with deep devotion brings immense joy. Their meditation on the divine, combined with yearning to see god, adds a graceful touch to their singing. In the soothing melodies of their musical offerings, they lose awareness of their own bodies, and we, too, lose ourselves in their divine music, experiencing naada brahman.

Giving to those seeking Uncha vritti or Bhiksha is considered a noble act. Uncha vritti involves living by gathering leftover grains in fields after the harvest, while Bhiksha is food obtained by asking for alms—a tradition practiced by pious souls. Usually, it's the meal served to a sadhu or monk visiting a household.

Once, a childless king sought guidance from sage Narada about having progeny. Brahma, the Creator, revealed there was no possibility. Accepting his fate, the king arranged a Ramayana katha ganam, honoring the scholar who suggested that welcoming someone seeking Unchavritti brings immense benefits, protecting 21 generations. Following this advice, the queen welcomed a person seeking Unchavritti with tears, and despite Brahma's prediction, she conceived.

Narada questioned Brahma about this apparent contradiction, considering karma's unyielding nature. Brahma explained that honoring the Ramayana katha ganam pleased God by uttering the divine name, thereby destroying the king's and queen's sins.

Saint Tyagaraja embarked on the sacred path of "Unchavritti," a choice revered by pious souls. Just a few steps from his house, a group of eager-hearted households awaited, ready to offer Bhiksha. As he walked a few steps, the very air seemed to shimmer with anticipation of beautiful songs composed by him. Those fortunate witnesses were spellbound, their souls entranced by the celestial melody that flowed from Tyagaraja's songs. These songs were different from Kritis and were perfect for group singing. As he went around some of the streets in the town, people would join him, singing along with him the glory of Lord Rama.

Saint Thyagaraja composed many divyanama and utsava sampradaya songs on Lord Rama. I will mention a few of the songs.

"Meluko dayanidhi" in Sourastra raga, "Melukovayya" in Bouli raga are wake up songs for Lord Sri Rama.

"Seetha kalyana vaibhogame" in Kuranji raga is sung during the wedding ceremony of Lord Rama and Sita in a temple.

"Koluvai unnade Kodandapani" in Devagandhari raga describes the beauty of Lord Rama sitting on the throne with Sita.

"Hecharika garara Hey ramachandra" in Yadukula kambhoji is sung to invite Lord Rama during the ceremony.

"Patiki harathire" is the harathi offering to Lord Sri Rama in Surati raga.

"Laliyugave" in Neelambari raga is sung in pavalimpu seva, which means to sing the Lord Sleep as a part of daily sevas.

Other songs include, "Rama kodanda raama" – Bhairavi raga.

"Ksheera sagara vihara" in AnandaBhairavi raga, "Napali sreerama" in Sankarabharanam raga, "Nagumomu galavani" in Madhyamavathi raga are some of the rare gems composed by saint Tyagaraja.

Tyagaraja and fellow devotees of Lord Hari would melodiously render these Keertanas in the mornings on the streets of Tiruvayyaru. Recollecting these songs in Thiruvaiyaru filled me with joy.

Harilo Ranga Hari

Makar Sankranti is a festival I eagerly looked forward to in my childhood. In Tamil Nadu, it's called Pongal; in Gujarat, it's known as Uttarayan. The most exciting part was my mother's beautiful drawings on the ground, known as "muggu" or "Rangoli" in Telugu. I loved adding different colors to make them even more vibrant.

Our home looked festive with those colorful patterns on the ground. Also, these small piles of cow dung called "gobbemma" represented the gopis waiting for Sri Krishna. Gobbemmalu are decorated with pumpkin flowers. Gopi + bommalu were called "gobbemmalu." The larger gobbemma was worshipped as Godadevi, the great devotee of Lord Krishna. Women used to walk around the gobbemma in groups, seeking the grace of Lord Krishna.

This festival marks the harvest season and involves using main crops such as sugarcane, rice, and wheat in the festivities. On Makar Sankranti, families came together, admiring the pretty designs and enjoying delicious food. It wasn't just about celebrating; it was a day to be thankful for nature and to spend time with our loved ones. The memories of those joyful moments during Makar Sankranti are like a treasure in my heart, reminding me of the simple joys found in family and traditions.

Amid the festive season, I would catch a peculiar sound, unlike anything I had heard before. It echoed from a distance, creating a unique rhythm that seemed to synchronize with the beating of my heart. Every day, I eagerly awaited this enchanting sound, especially during the chilly winter season in India.

One morning, wrapped in the cozy embrace of my winter sweater, I decided to follow the sound. As I ventured closer, the melody grew louder, weaving its way into the very fabric of the cold, crisp air. The anticipation within me intensified with each step.

To my surprise, the enchanting sound led me to a haridasu, a man incarnation of a great saint, Narada. His voice is sweet, and he plays Tanpura in such a perfect sruti that I forgot myself. The festive spirit enveloped the surroundings, creating a musical atmosphere filled with joy and warmth.

As I stood there, mesmerized by the beauty of his devotional songs, I realized that the sound was not just a melody; it was from a far-off planet that gives continuous joy, a celebration that touches the soul, a promise to self-realization.

My mother would call out urgently, telling me to give some rice to haridasu. Since he moves swiftly to other houses, he cannot wait for too long.

In the heart of devotion, there was a belief that If a home decorated with a muggu or rangoli belonged to true devotees, Lord Krishna would visit as a haridasu to bless them. The tambura bowl on his shoulder was like a sign, showing that Lord Vishnu was watching over and protecting the Earth. He bears akshaya patra on his head, which can give devotees unlimited blessings.

As the haridasu went from door to door, his soulful singing echoed hari nama sankeertan, emphasizing that everyone is equal in the eyes of the Lord. It was a simple yet powerful tradition, where every home became a sacred space, and the melody of devotion filled the air.

I always enjoyed listening to haridasu during the Sankranthi festival. He, the servant of Lord Vishnu, would wander around, playing the tambura and singing with perfect pitch. His melodious singing always caught my attention. I eagerly waited for him because my mother would give me rice and fruits to offer to him. Haridasu visited every house during the Sankranthi festival. He was a scholar in Sanskrit and sang songs about the Bhagavatam.

Bliss experienced at the physical level is referred to as "Manavaanandam." For instance, acquiring a smartphone can bring about a form of happiness known as "Manavaanandam," representing the fundamental joy that humans experience. Progressing to the next level, there is "chittanandam," the joy derived from mental processes such as thinking or enjoying. The highest level is "chidanandam," a combination of "chit" (consciousness) and "ananda" (bliss), representing the happiness of the soul. At this profound level, one can transcend the limitations of the body and mind.

I think I used to get such a joy of ecstasy, "chidanandam," especially when immersed in uplifting music. Haridas, among others, inspired me to explore various music artists. I am sure most music lovers and performers get this type of happiness.

Haridasu sweetly sings "Harilo ranga hari," casting a tranquil aura over those in his vicinity.

Harikatha

Harikatha is a traditional Indian storytelling art form that combines the elements of music, narration, and devotional discourse. The term "Harikatha" translates to "stories of Lord Hari," with "Hari" being one of the many names of the god Vishnu. This cultural and spiritual tradition has deep roots in South India, particularly in states like Andhra Pradesh, Karnataka, Tamil Nadu, and Telangana.

In a Harikatha performance, a skilled narrator, often called the "Harikatha artist" or "Haridasa," weaves intricate narratives from Hindu mythology, epics, and Puranas together. The stories are typically centered around the divine exploits of gods and goddesses, emphasizing moral and ethical lessons. The narrator employs a blend of classical and devotional music to enhance the emotional and spiritual impact of the performance.

Ajjada Adibhatla Narayana Dasu holds the esteemed position of being the pioneer of the Telugu Harikatha tradition. A highly skilled singer, he possessed extensive knowledge of ragas and the principles of sangeetha shastra. Additionally, he showcased his prowess as a proficient poet, demonstrating fluency in numerous languages and exhibiting expertise in dance. He could do talam by using both hands, two legs, and his head, all while singing in the intricate patterns of raga, tala, natya, and bhava. His profound contributions, through creating Kavyas (poetry) and Prabandhas (compositions), have elevated Harikatha to a distinctive and revered art form within the Telugu cultural landscape.

In recognizing and celebrating the contributions of Narayana Dasu, the Telugu Harikatha tradition stands as a unique art form that is rarely performed in the world. It remains an integral part of the cultural heritage, offering a profound and enriching experience for those who participate in or appreciate the art form.

Grand Sire (Pitamaha) of Carnatic Music

Purandara Dasa, a prosperous merchant in gold, silver, and various jewelry in Karnataka, gave away all his wealth to become a Haridasa.

At 30, he understood the emptiness of chasing after material wealth and greed, so he let go of his desire for riches. Spiritual wisdom illuminated his path. He journeyed across Karnataka, visiting sacred places and eventually became a disciple of Sage Vyasa Teertha, earning the name Purandara Dasa. During his travels, he composed heartfelt songs called "Devaranamas," praising Lord Hari, also known as Vitthala. Songs like "Bhagyada Lakshmee Baramma," "Jagadoddharana," "Venkatachala Nilayam", "Ranga baro", "Sakalagraha", "Kelano hari talano", "Innudaya bharade" by Purandara Dasa are sweet melodies.

He introduced mayamalavagowla raga for the beginners of Carnatic music. He introduced basic exercises saraliswara, jantaswara, and other exercises. Purandara Dasa is recognized as the Grand Sire (Pitamaha) of Carnatic music.

One of his geethams "Keraya niranu" in soothing malahari raga, he says – "*Just like taking water from a pond and offering it back, you live life by submitting yourself to Lord Hari as gratitude.*" Showing gratitude to God is saranagathi. Purandaradasar's songs have a feeling of never leaving the lotus feet of heart and listeners always drench in the bhakti tatva of the great composer.

In another geetham called "Padumanabha Paramapurusha" in the Malahari raga, Purandaradasa describes Lord Hari as "Udadhi Nivasa Uraga Sayana," meaning He dwells on the ocean, reclining on the Adisesha serpent. This phrase resembles Saint Tyagaraja's "Ksheera Sagara Sayana," where the Lord reclines on the milky ocean. It seems great thinkers like Saint Tyagaraja and Purandaradasa share similar thoughts, promising to immerse us in devotion.

Swami Haridas, the Guru of the renowned musician Tansen was a desciple of Purandara Dasa..

Ramadasu

There was a story of a boy, who lived in a small village in Andhra Pradesh. One day, he discovered a beautiful parrot that captivated him, prompting him to bring it home. Excited, he kept the parrot in a cage. He enjoyed observing it daily. However, the bird seemed miserable, longing to return home. Each day, the parrot sang, "Rama, Rama, Rama, Rama...," and the boy was delighted in its sweet voice. After 12 days, he felt sympathy for the parrot and set it free. The bird flew away happily, reuniting with its family.

As time passed, the boy was reborn as Kancherla Gopanna in the year 1620 C.E., born in a simple Brahmin family in Nelakondapalli, Northern Andhra Pradesh. His parents were Linganna Murthy and Kamamba.

His uncle, who served as a minister to King Taane Shah of Golconda, assigned him the role of a revenue officer in Bhadrachalam. A few years later, Kancherla Gopanna visited Bhadrachalam for a fair. He also wanted to see the holy Parnasala, where Rama had stayed with Sita and Lakshmana during his exile. Near Bhadrachalam, there was another site where Shabari had lived before attaining moksha from Lord Rama. However, when Kancherla Gopanna saw the temple of Lord Rama, which held great significance for many, he was disappointed. The temple, where Potana had received darshan from Rama to write the Bhagavatham, was not in a good condition. No priests performed puja in the temple, and the people completely neglected it.

Kancherla Gopanna decided to gather funds and personally oversee the temple's reconstruction, involving the community. People contributed various items such as gold necklaces, bangles, rings, coins, and more for the rebuilding of the temple. With these donations combined with Kancherla Gopanna's wealth, a substantial sum of money was collected. But this was not enough to construct the temple. People requested him to continue constructing the temple. People said that they could contribute once their crops yielded. He borrowed money from the nawab's tax revenue to provide an abode for his deity, promising to repay Gopanna's borrowed sum. Nawab was furious and ordered to put Gopanna in jail for twelve years. Gopanna sang so many songs on Lord Rama. His songs are sweet melodies showering a lot of love on Lord Rama. "Paluke bangara mayena kodandapani," "Pahi rama prabho," "Taraka mantramu," "Takkuvemi manaku," "Eteeru gananu daya," "Yemayya rama" are few of them that melted the hearts of the listeners. Kancharla Gopanna was later known as Ramadasu, one of the great devotees of Lord Rama.

Rama and Lakshmana, appearing as two young men, settled his debts and released him from jail. The golden coins offered by Sri Rama are recognized as Ram Tanka coins. Remarkably, these coins are still visible today at Sri Sita Ramachandra

Swamy Vaari Devasthanam in Bhadrachalam. The nawab acknowledged the greatness of Ramadas and promptly released him, even granting him land around Bhadrachalam to continue his devoted service to Lord Rama.

Ramadasu had inspired many saints and devotees with his songs and devotion. Saint Tyagaraja is one among them. In saint Tyagaraja's kriti "Kaligiyunte kada" in Keeravani ragam, he mentions – I admire Sri Ramadasa, the supreme devotee of Lord Ramachandra, who shines and showers grace from Bhadrachalam in this Kali Yuga.

Ramadasu, in one of his songs "Idgo bhadradri gautami adigo chudandi" describes "Bhadrachalam" where he built the temple. Bhadrachalam is the magnificent abode of Lord Rama and Sita. Look at this beautiful place delightfully. Worship Lord Rama with devotion.

"Haridasu" usually refers to a dedicated singer or servant of God who expresses love and devotion through devotional songs. Many musicians who embraced the path of bhakti yoga achieved liberation, and their songs had a mesmerizing effect, allowing listeners to forget themselves in the nectar of the music.

CHAPTER 13

MADHURAM

*A*midst the towering mountains there lies a legacy woven with the melodies of divine inspiration. These majestic peaks of Kaliyuga Vaikunta, with their grandeur, serve as the backdrop for the sacred compositions of the legendary composers who live on with their timeless melodies.

Annamayya was a great devotee of Lord Venkateswara. Annamayya was an enlightened musician who wrote many songs in Telugu. He is known as "Pada Kavitha Pitamaha". He used as many words as possible in Telugu, which is a rare feat for any musician.

As a child, he would correct the melody and rhythm of singers who couldn't sing properly. When Annamayya was eight years old, he followed a group of pilgrims from his village, Tallapaka, to Tirupati and then to Tirumala. The seven peaks are Sheshadri, Vedadri,

Garudadri, Anjanadri, Vrishabhadri, Narayanadri, and Venkatadri. He gazed at the splendid peaks of the Tirumala hills, looking like a transformed hood of Adisesha for Lord Venkateswara. Overwhelmed with joy, he began singing with bliss.

His song, "Adivo alladivo," echoed through the hills, melting the hearts of the devotees. Climbing to a breathtaking Anjanadri hill, he continued to sing, his voice blending with the rustling leaves and the whispers of the wind. The young boy got tired, he rested in bamboo groves, where Goddess Alamelu Manga appeared.

Goddess Alamelu Manga blessed him and revealed the sacredness of Tirumala Hill formed from the Salagrama rock. Annamayya removed his footwear, upon witnessing the divine everywhere. He proceeded to the Pushkarini, took a bath, and felt rejuvenated. Offering prayers to Lord Varaha, he walked around the temple with Champaka Pradakshinam and entered the temple.

Upon seeing Lord Venkateswara, Annamayya's heart filled with a rare joy. The magnificent idol of the Lord was breathtaking. Temple priests loved his songs and blessed the boy.

At once, a beautiful song emerged from his voice – "Podaganti mayya mimmu purushottama."

He wrote many songs in ecstasy, expressing his extraordinary devotion. He composed a song every day, wandering from place to place.

"Chandamama Ravo..Jabilli ravo"

"Srimannarayana"

"Brahma kadigina padamu"

"Jo achyutananda"

"Deva devam bhaje"

"Cheri yasodaku"

"Dolayam"

"Entamatramuna"

"Nanati batuku"

In Tirumala, there lived a Vaishnava sage named Ghana Vishnu. He was a great devotee and a wise man who shared the teachings of Vaishnava philosophy with those who sought his guidance. One night, on the auspicious day of "Dwadasi," Lord Venkateswara appeared in Ghana Vishnu's dream.

In his dream, the Lord said, "Tomorrow, a pious soul named Annamayya will come to you. He is dark and handsome, constantly singing songs about me. Mark his shoulders with the conch shell and the wheel, this is my blessing."

The following day, Ghanavishnu eagerly awaited at the temple's ‹Yagasala' after performing his ablutions. Holding the sacred signets of Lord Vishnu, he watched for the arrival of Annamayya.

Soon enough, Annamayya arrived at the temple, singing the praises of Lord Hari. Ghanavishnu, recognizing the boy, approached him, ready to fulfill the divine instruction given in the dream. Annamayya gracefully obliged Lord Venkateswara's blessings and transformed himself as Srivaishnava, from Annamayya to Annamacharya.

Annamayya introduced various ritual offerings in Tirumala, such as Abhishekam darshan and Brahmotsavam (festival). Abhishekham is performed every week on Friday at 7 am IST in Tirumala. The Abhishekam starts with water from Akasa Ganga Theertham, followed by milk, and other fragrances.

Annamacharya sang a beautiful song during the Abhishekam, titled "Kanti sukravaramu gadiya ledinta," composed in the Anandabhairavi ragam. Annamacharya described witnessing Sri Venkatesa during the Abhishekam, where the Lord, resembling a bumble bee, had golden bowls filled with Pachcha Karpooram (camphor) powder applied to his body. The usual Chandanam (sandalwood), Camphor powder, Saffron paste, and other fragrant substances were used.

After the bath, the Lord, adorned in a dhoti, shines like the ever-fresh jasmine.

Devotees gazed with wonder at the sight, as the ritual included the use of a few drops of sweat from the Civet cat (punugu pilli), adding a delightful fragrance. Annamacharya mentioned that Lord Venkateswara also enjoyed observing and amusing himself along with his devotees.

He penned 32,000 songs, but only 12,000 are available today. His additional writings, including "Dwipada Ramayana," "Venkatachala Mahatmyam," "Sankirtana Lakshanam," and a few more works in other languages, have been lost.

One day, Annamacharya spoke to his son Peda Tirumalaiah privately, saying, "Timmappa, my life is ending. You must continue my mission of composing a new song for Lord Srinivasa daily." He handed his tambura to his son. In 1503, during Bahula Dwadasi in the Dundubhi month, Annamacharya, aged 95, passed away. On this holy day, Annamayya's son, Pedda Tirumalaiah, sang "Dinamu dwadasi nedu" (Today is Dwadasi) song. We are all successors and heirs of Annamacharya's great musical legacy. His Sankeertanas are a feast for music listeners. His songs enlighten, energize, and entertain us.

Taragnam

Another legendary composer was Narayana Theertha. He was a saint and a scholar. His iconic collections of tarangams in "Sri Krishna Leela Tarangini" are widely known today among music lovers. It contains 12 chapters. His songs are full of love towards Lord Krishna, and his madhura bhakti is very inspiring. "Tarangam" was born in his voice. People who listen to these songs are thrilled with Sanskrit's beautiful use and the divinity in his songs. The listeners experience spiritual ecstasy while listening to the tarangams. He traveled across India with his disciples, spreading knowledge of the scriptures and teaching people how to attain mukti. He attained jeeva samadhi in a village called Thirupoonthuruthi near Thanjavur.

Some of the songs are – "Alokaye sri Balakrishnam"

आलोकये श्री बालकृष्णम - सखि आनंद सुंदर ताण्डव कृष्णम

Some of the stanzas of the song as below.

नवनीत खण्ड दधिचोर कृष्णं भक्त

भव पाश बन्ध मोचन कृष्णम्

चरण नकि्वणति नूपुर कृष्णं - कर

संगत कनक कंकण कृष्णं।

किंकिनी जाल घण घणति कृष्णं - लोक
संकति तारावली मौक्तिक कृष्णं।
सुंदर नासा मौक्तिक शोभति कृष्णं-नंद
नंदन मखंड विभूति कृष्णं।
नंद सुनंदादिवंदति कृष्णं-श्री
नारायण तीर्थ वरद कृष्णं।

His other songs include

"Madhava mavama deva krishna"

"Parama karunaya"

"Sri nilayam sakhi Sri nilayam"

"Pahi pahi mohana krishna"

"Kalaya kalyanani narayana"

Jayadeva

The poet Sri Jayadeva was born in the 11th century. He was born in Bindu Bilva village near the Puri Jagannath Temple in Orissa. The divine love of Sri Radha-Krishna resides in Sri Jayadeva's musical heart. Poet Jayadeva's "Gita Govinda" is one of the most famous compositions in the Sanskrit language which has lyrical excellence and exhibits "madhura bhakti". Krishna's dancing, singing, and merrymaking with this unique group of milkmaids is known as "Rasa lila," (or) "Rasa krida." It involves dancing in a circle, accompanied by the Gopis singing to Krishna's raga coming from his flute. This enchanting event takes place exclusively in Vrindavan. Gopis, in Brindavan, are not mere milkmaids. They are all saints and sages in their earlier incarnations, as per the tradition. Krishna desires to satisfy every soul based on their proximity to him.

"Gita Govinda" work is a lyrical poetry divided into "Prabandham." These prabandham contain couplets grouped into eights called "Ashtapadis."

The poems vividly depict the "Madhura bhakti" – the attraction between Radha and Krishna, their separation, their yearning and union with the

Paramatma, the supreme soul. Jayadeva's Ashtapadis lyrical excellence, exquisite vocabulary, and divine love have a unique place in literature.

Jayadeva took inspiration from various iconic writers. Valmiki inspires the design, melodrama, and anguish in the separation of the lead characters. Bharata Muni contributes to dance dramas, while Kalidasa influences the word selection, brevity, and the use of small words with significant meanings. Jayadeva himself sets trends in language, grammar, and poetic aesthetics.

Kshetrayya, a renowned composer and poet from the 17th century, wrote numerous padams in Telugu, with "Madhura Bhakti" as the main theme, expressing his intense devotion to Lord Muvva Gopala (Lord Krishna) in his native village Muvva, Andhra Pradesh.

There are many composers who truly created a blissful experience with their compositions.

My guruji, Sri Dr. Nookala Chinna Satyanarayana, composed the song "Srinivasa Varadayaka" in Natakuranji raga during his walk by foot from Tirupati to Tirumala. Upon reaching the sanctum sanctorum of Tirumala, he sang the composition that he had composed during his journey on foot from Tirupati. On another occasion, I had the privilege of walking along with my guruji from Tirupati to Tirumala, and it turned into a truly musical experience. I accompanied him singing numerous songs, creating memorable moments in my life.

CHAPTER 14

THE FLOAT FESTIVAL

*I*ndia celebrates numerous festivals across the country. In South India, people mark special days for festivals like New Year, Vaikunta Ekadasi, Pongal, Diwali, and more. Additionally, there are celebrations like housewarming, birthdays, Shasti Poorthi (60th birthday) both at family and community levels.

The Tyagaraja Swamy temple complex has shrines, mandapas, temple gardens, Gopura entrances, and a stone chariot.

The grand chariot festival occurs each year in April–May, coinciding with the Tamil month of Chitrai. The colossal chariot, weighing 300 tonnes and towering at 96 ft (29 m), is one of the largest in Asia and India, making its way through the temple's four main streets during the festive celebration. The annual temple car festival (chariot) and floating festival (theppam) attract thousands of devotees.

The chariot festival is a unique celebration that involves people from various communities. It brings together individuals from surrounding areas to participate, enjoy, and worship the deity. That's why the temple or car festival is commonly called "thiruvizha," meaning a holy celebration.

South India developed a system of water harvesting using reservoirs or tanks, which served as sources for drinking and domestic use. In the Mahabharata, sage Narada advised Yudhishthira to dig large lakes to store water, making cultivation less dependent on rainwater. Around 300 B.C., Kautilya, in his Arthashastra, discussed state assistance for irrigation. Every temple has a tank (pond). The temple tanks were central to all activities, providing water for the deity's ritual bath (abhishekham) and the devotees' bathing. Festivals revolved around the tanks, with a mandapam at the center hosting the deity during the float festivals (theppam).

Temples in India have a rich tradition of weaving music into their rituals and festivities. These sacred spaces have inspired the creation of devotional compositions, like bhajans, kirtans, or keertanas, dedicated to specific deities. Music has historically thrived under the patronage of temples, with kings and wealthy individuals supporting musicians and composers. Some temples continue this tradition, fostering the growth and preservation of Indian classical music.

While the Thyagaraja temple's roots trace back to the Pallavas, evidenced by Saptamatrika figures, its artistic and architectural evolution aligns with the Chola, Vijayanagara, and Maratha periods.

During the festival, the chariot travels around the four main streets in Tiruvarur, surrounding the temple. This event attracts thousands of people from all over Tamil Nadu. Following the chariot festival is the "Theppam," which means float festival. The float festival is also called Teppotsavam. In Tiruvarur it is called Kamalalayam Float (Theppam) festival. As part of this festival, they decorate the temple's main idol and take it in a procession through the temple tank. The float circles Kamalalayam three times in the night.In the tranquil setting, the gopuram's reflection shimmers in the water.

Being in the audience at the Thiruvarur Tyagaraja Swamy Theppam Thiruvizha music concert is truly amazing. The electrifying atmosphere at the festival is indescribable. According to the temple authorities, over three lakh devotees visit the Theppam festival in the evening. I feel fortunate to witness the beautiful sight of the deity adorned in grand festive Alankaaram. I boarded the float. I was surrounded by water in the tank, and the lit lamps created a jubilant, divine atmosphere. The deities were taken in the decorated float.

Typically, a vocal and Nadaswaram concert were held on the float itself. The vocal music concert was about to start. The violinist and mridangists were ready to play. The singer had set her pitch-perfect sruti, creating a holy atmosphere. She started the popular Hamsadhwani ragam. Seated in the audience, I soaked in the melody. The vocalist's resonant voice and adept raga command created a captivating music flow. After the singer completed the rendition of the raga, the violinist, playing like the great M. S. Gopala Krishnan, stole our hearts. The performance unfolded and connecting the audience to the spiritual essence of the moment.

The vocal artist rendered the kriti "Vatapi Ganapatim bhajeham" in the raga composed by the renowned Muthuswami Dikshitar. This musical experience instantly took me to Badami, Karnataka, the ancient town once called Vatapi. There, you find religious monuments dating back over 1300 years to the era of the Chalukya kings, bringing forth vivid memories of the Lord Ganesha idol. Among these, the

"Lower Shivalaya," a captivating temple from the 7th century, stands out.

The raga awakens the essence of devotion, a bhakti rasa. It emerges from the foundational scale (melakarta) known as dheera sankarabharanam. The raga has an uplifting and refreshing nature. Hamsadhwani is an excellent choice to begin any concert. It is a perfect opener. This reminds me that Hamsadhwani is fondly called vighneswara raga. Derived from dheera sankarabharam, the Hamsadhwani raga belongs to Lord Shiva's musical family.

Hamsadhwani means the sound of a swan. Swan (hamsa) is a spiritual symbol in India known for its purest form of wisdom. The terms "so" and "hm" represent the process of breathing, signifying both inhalation and exhalation, forming "hamsa." Paramahamsa is the title of honor given to spiritual teachers who follow Sanathana Dharma and attain enlightenment. In ancient Greece, the swan was regarded as a symbol of beauty and grace. It held a special significance and was considered sacred to the goddess Aphrodite, representing her divine qualities. In Greek mythology, the swan was also revered by Apollo, the god associated with music and other domains. In Greek mythology, the swan held a similar significance, symbolizing beauty and grace, sacred to the goddess Aphrodite and revered by Apollo, the god of music. It's fascinating how these ancient connections bridge cultures and bring depth to the composition, infusing the music with layers of cultural and spiritual significance.

The swan serves as the divine vehicle for Goddess Saraswati and is renowned for its ability to discern between water and milk. This capacity to discriminate between substances represents its association with wisdom, education, and the ability to differentiate between what is good and what is not.

Hamsadhwani is recognized by the same name in Hindustani and Carnatic music traditions.

As the performance unfolds, gamakas of the notes carry the essence of meditation on Hamsadhwani raga, a musical journey that transcends time and space.

The float festival is a magnificent sight. I believe I am in one of India's largest temple tanks. The water is so clean that it seems to be supplied by a continuous source.

I remember the yearly Theppotsavam (Float festival) of Lord Venkateswara at Tirumala. The "Pushkarini" was Vishnu's heavenly tank in Vaikuntam, brought to earth by the eagle Garuda for Vishnu's use. It is located in front of the Tirumala temple and is considered equivalent to the Ganga and other sacred rivers. Seventeen holy waters, or tirthas, are believed to converge in the Swami Pushkarini.

According to the Varaha Purana, Lord Rama's success in his battle with Ravana is attributed to bathing in the Swami Pushkarini, as it grants success to all who bathe in it. The Rishi Narayana, after whom the hill was named Narayanadri, regularly bathed in the tank and meditated on its banks.

It is said that Annamayya embarked on a journey to visit all the ponds up the Tirumala hills. He encountered Kumaradhara, where Kumaraswami, the son of Shiva, had performed penance to cleanse himself of the sin of defeating a demon named Tarakasura. Annamayya then visited Amarathirtha, a place where gods bathe daily. He also saw "Akasaganga," where Anjana underwent a twelve-year penance before giving birth to Anjaneya.

I heard another kriti performed by the musician at the concert. "Upachaaramu chekonavayya uraga raaja sayana"

The saint Tyagaraja pleads with the Lord, who reclines on the the mighty serpent (seshasaayi) to accept his offerings.

"Shodasa Upachar" is a complete worship ritual known as pooja. The term "Upachar" means service, and there are 16 steps involved in this worship process.

Typically accompanied by Vedic chantings, it can be performed mentally with closed eyes (manasa puja). This "Shodasha Upachara Pooja" is a common practice in temples and homes on special occasions.

These 16 steps symbolically represent various ways of expressing reverence, such as offering a golden throne for the deity to sit on, washing their feet and hands, providing water to drink, ceremonially bathing with sacred waters, offering new clothes, applying sandal paste and perfumes, adorning with jewels, worshiping with flowers, presenting fragrant incense, lighting a lamp, offering food (Prasada), fruits, and sweet drinks, chanting praises, performing Arati, and finally, prostrating and seeking blessings.

In one of the charanam he mentions – "kapaTa nATaka sootradhArivai

kAmita phalamosagE Rama"

"Oh Rama, you are the enigmatic director of the drama of the world. You grant the fruits of our desires."

The float festival indicates that the pond is bhava sagaram, the sea of difficulties in life. The float (theppam) is the body. The deity in the float is the god who removes difficulties in life.

Annamacharya expresses, "Tolliyunu marraku," "Teppaga marraku meeda telugu vadu" envisioning Krishna as the divine child, lying on a banyan leaf and floating on the ocean.

According to tradition, at the end of a creation cycle, the heat from the sun god Surya turns everything on Earth to ashes. This lasts for eight thousand yugas. Then, the wind god Vayu blows continuously, forming huge clouds. Incessant rain leads to a great flood, submerging the entire earth for millions of years. The Child form of Vishnu (Krishna) rests on a Ficus Leaf known as Vatapatra Shayee on this water. Symbolically, it signifies the first form of life on earth. This extraordinary incident is narrated in the Markandeya Purana.

Markandeya Rishi was blessed to witness the severe flood. He saw destruction everywhere, with water submerging everything for millions of years. Eventually, he noticed Krishna, in the form of a child, floating on a ficus leaf. The baby Krishna was lying on the leaf, sucking his toe.

Approaching closer, Markandeya saw the baby take a breath, and he was drawn inside. Within, the Rishi witnessed thousands of universes and a myriad of living forms. When the baby exhaled, the Rishi returned to Earth.

Annamacharya describes the waves of the river Kaveri as gentle arms swaying the banyan leaf cradle. The god, in the form of a child, looks charming. The swing and song bring him comfort.

South Indian music underwent a transformative evolution with the arrival of musical maestros such as Tyagaraja, Muthuswamy Dikshitar, and Syama Sastri. This musical era, spanning the late 18th and early 19th centuries, witnessed a profound shift in the landscape of Carnatic music. These legendary composers enriched the Carnatic music and cultural fabric of their time. Their collective influence paved the way for a new chapter in the history of South Indian classical music, shaping melodies and lyrical expressions for generations to come.

The waters of the Thyagaraja temple resonated with applause. The song concludes by expressing *"Oh Lord Rama, you deserve the fragrance of various flowers like jaji, sampangi, maravamu, virajaji, and kuruveru."*

Good music brings tears to eyes, touches the soul, and fills listeners with inexplicable bliss.

The mridangam artist concluded the tani avartanam after the singer finished the swara kalpana, the spontaneous notes in the bhairavi raga.

The mridangam and violin player nicely accompanied the vocalist, who was singing joyfully. The artists felt it was a really proud moment for them.

The audience appreciated and enjoyed the music performance so much that they asked for an encore of some of the songs. The artist was more than delighted to honor their wishes.

The singer wrapped up the concert with "pavamAna sutuDu paTTu pAdAravindamulaku." This Kruti is often performed as the "Mangalam," marking the end of a Carnatic concert. "*Oh, Sri Rama, may there be everlasting auspiciousness and victory to your sacred name and appearance*." I experienced the bliss of listening to the music concert. It conveys that happiness comes from knowledge, and connecting with the divine (Brahman). Understanding ragas and having love for God can guide us on the path of righteousness.

God delights in songs. The god, known as "Samagana Lola," takes pleasure in sama gana, derived from the Vedas.

Great musical pieces have a lasting impact on our minds, often causing musicians and music enthusiasts to think deeply as they remain captivated by the melodies. It is said that the legendary musician Dr. Sripada Pinakapani experienced this firsthand when he attended a vocal concert by Musiri Subramanya Iyer.

During the performance, Musiri sang a Tyagaraja kriti "Enta Vedukondu Raghava" in the Saraswati Manohari raga, leaving a profound impact on Dr. Pinakapani.

The song haunted him for days, serving as a lasting influence on his musical journey. Carnatic music, also known as "Karnataka Sangeetham," is defined as "Karneshu atathi ithi Karnatakaha," which means that when we listen to any beautiful music and it delights our ears, it is referred to as Carnatic music.

The rich music culture, and spiritual treasures of India need preservation and passing on to the next generations. When music becomes bliss, so does the raga. No matter which raga resonates with our hearts, we can seek it wholeheartedly, with the awareness that eventual union with the divine will satisfy us in a way that nothing else can.

***

Echoes Of Ragas: Exploring Listener's Choice

Stars twinkle in the vast sky, telling tales of distant worlds. Their celestial nectar, carried by melodies, descends to Earth, touching every soul with the magic of the cosmos.

In one of Tyagaraja's songs, he portrays Lord Rama as the Aarabhi raga. Tyagaraja envisions the Lord as the embodiment of music, describing how Lord Rama descended as the nectar of music with the enchanting ragas that captivate the hearts of the devotees.

A song is usually called a "Kriti" or "Keertana" in Carnatic music. In classical Indian music, a Kriti typically features an "Anu Pallavi" – an extension of the main Pallavi, which serves as the song's central theme. On the other hand, a Keertana also consists of

Charanams, representing the stanzas or verses of the composition.

Tyagaraja, immersed in the devotion of Lord Rama, composed the kriti "Naada Sudha rasambilanu Naraakritaayera.. Pranava" (as we repeat the pallavi of the song it is sung as "Pranava nAda sudhA rasambilanu") in Aarabhi raga.

Tyagaraja says – "OM" has become Lord Rama.

The Nada is the basis of Vedas, scriptures, epics, and all the knowledge. He adds that Lord Rama's bow is embellished with seven bells, each representing a musical note: Sa, Ri, Ga, Ma, Pa, Da, Ni.

Lord Rama's bow is called the "Kodanda." The mantra "Shri Rama Jaya Rama Kodhanda Rama" is a prayer praising Lord Rama and his powerful bow Kodhanda, which signifies victory for the Lord, recognizing the strength and triumph associated with the divine bow. The pairing of Rama with Kodanda symbolizes invincibility and the ability to overcome challenges. Saint Tyagaraja depicts Lord Rama's bow as a wonderful raga in its own right. Rama's bow embodies the essence of a musical raga. This special bow, Kodhanda, is more than just a weapon – it's a melody. The Kodanda bow vibrates when the lord applies it. The sound produced from the bow has become a creation – a raga.

The song says "Dura naya desyamu trigunamu Niratagati sharamulu ra" – the arrows it shoots create showers of different types of ragas – Ghana, Naya, and Desya ragas. We are all engrossed in the nectar of melodies created by the ragas.

Raga is the essence of Indian music. Without raga, there is no Indian music. Ragas are formed using Swaras. Swaras are the individual notes in a raga.

Indian classical music is a spontaneous and captivating art form that transports the listener through the flow of its notes. It is a medium through which the soul connects. Indian music not only entertains the mind but also enlightens the soul. If we liken the game of chess to music, the melody becomes the king, holding the utmost importance in the musical realm. With their specific rules and intricate oscillations known as gamakas, ragas define the world of South Indian music. The gamakas, with their subtle nuances, enhance the listener's experience, adding depth and richness to the music.

In South Indian classical music, expressions and dynamics play a pivotal role, defining the unique combination of swaras.

Within the Indian classical music, The seven swaras hold significance, with the Tonic (Sa) and Dominant (Pa) remaining fixed. However, it is worth noting that the Pa note may not be present in certain ragas.

The Ri note can be classified as Shudhdha Rishabha and Chathushruthi Rishabha. The Ga note can be further categorized into Sadharana Gandhara and Anthara Gandhara. The Ma note has two classifications: Shudhdha Madhyama and Prati Madhyama. The Dha note also has two classifications: Shudhdha Dhaivatha and Chathushruthi Dhaivatha. Lastly, the Ni note can be classified as Kaishika Nishadha and N2 Kaakali Nishadha. There are other types of vikruti swaras, and anya swara (additional notes) as well. With all these combinations of different types of notes, the ragas are formed.

The melodic rendition of compositions involves improvisation and the exploration of various ragas (melodic scales) and tala (rhythmic cycles).

According to the Natya Shastra, there are nine primary rasa called "NAVARASA:"

- Shringara Rasa: The sentiment of love, romance, and beauty.
- Hasya Rasa: The sentiment of humor, laughter, and joy.
- Karuna Rasa: The sentiment of compassion, empathy, and sadness.

- Raudra Rasa: The sentiment of anger, fury, and violence.
- Veera Rasa: The sentiment of heroism, courage, and valor.
- Bhayanaka Rasa: The sentiment of fear, terror, and awe.
- Bibhatsa Rasa: The sentiment of disgust, revulsion, and loathing.
- Adbhuta Rasa: The sentiment of wonder, amazement, and astonishment.
- Shanta Rasa: The sentiment of tranquillity, peace, and serenity.

Sound carries vibrations that can manifest in various forms. Gamakas emerge from these vibrations. Gamakas occupy a vital place in Carnatic music. They define the characteristics of the raga. The personality of the raga is understood through the gamakas.

What is a "gamaka" ? – We can call it a charming shake of the note. Gamaka is a refinement of sound, a grace that adorns a song. It is like an ornament to a musical note.

Gamaka is as old as the Vedas, and it was the dominant feature of the Samaveda.

A raga has the power to bring about different complex emotions, which are evident in Tyagaraja Swamy kritis. Raga is created by self-expression called mano dharma and shaped by the inevitable aesthetic laws. Ragas are vehicles of emotion and the power of expression. A brilliant musician communicates this concept to the audience through their unique interpretation.

Please note that S (Shadjam) and P (Panchamam) notes in the arohana and avarohana do not change because of a fixed scale called Sruti. Indian classical music follows a fixed scale approach where S and P sound like constants. The other swara sthana (particular swara) we need to refer to are given below.

R1 – Suddha Rishabham, R2 – Chatusruthi Rishabham

G1 – Sadharana Gandharam, G2 – Antara Gandharam

M1 – Suddha Madhyamam, M2 – Prati Madhyamam

D1 – Suddha Dhaivatam, D2 – Chatusruti Dhaivatam

N1 – Kaishika Nishadam, N2 – Kakali Nishadam

In the 13th century, Sarngadeva authored "Sangita Ratnakara," a Sanskrit music book detailing the ten primary gamakas in music. The ten gamakas as follows:

1. Arohana: The swaras of a raga in ascending order. For example, a popular raga, Kalyani takes the order S, R2, G2, M2, P, D2, N2, S
2. Avarohana: The swaras of a raga in descending order. The same raga Kalyani takes the order S, N2, D2, P, M2, G2, R2, S
3. Dhalu: SR, SG, SM, SP... etc.
4. Sphurita:
   Sphurita is a significant aspect of South Indian music. Accentuating the second note in a sequence is called Sphuritam. For instance, when we take the pattern – SS RR GG, emphasizing the highlighted notes is known as sphuritam.
5. Kampita: MMMM, PPPP, DDDD, NNNN, etc.
6. Ahata: SR, RG, GM, MP, etc.
7. Pratyahata: SN, ND, DP, PM, etc.
8. Tripuccha: SSS, RRR, GGG, etc.
9. Andolita: SRS, PP, SRS, DD, etc.
10. Murchana: The use of the Arohana and avarohana as a phrase, at once. The personality of raga is embodied in murchana. Eg: SGMDNS and SNDMGS

Most musicians suggest fifteen types of gamakas that enhance the beauty of the raga rendition.

Rasa in the context of Sanskrit literature and aesthetics, refers to the different emotional and aesthetic moods or sentiments evoked in the audience or readers through various artistic expressions such as literature, drama, music, dance, and visual arts. The concept of rasas originated from the ancient Indian treatise on aesthetics called the Natya Shastra, attributed to the sage Bharata Muni.

In Indian classical music, certain ragas are associated with specific times of the day. In Hindustani classical music, the concept of "prahar" refers to dividing the 24-hour day into specific periods, each associated with a particular set of ragas. These prahars or time divisions help determine the appropriate ragas to be performed during specific times of the day. The "Ashta" means eight and "Prahar" refers to a period of 3 hours. Since a day is divided into 24 hours, it is also divided into eight prahars, each prahar spanning 3 hours. The duration from 6:00 PM in the evening to 6:00 AM the following day is known as "Ashta Prahar."

In other words, during the day, there are eight segments of time, each consisting of three hours, and the collective term for these eight segments is "Ashta Prahar." It helps in organizing and understanding the different time divisions within a 24-hour day. However, in the South Indian style of music, there is no specific division of time into praharas. Instead, ragas are often categorized based on the general time of day they are associated with. The broad categorizations include morning ragas, afternoon ragas, evening ragas, and night ragas.

In the above-mentioned kriti, the arrows shot from the Lord's bow create showers of different types of ragas.

Ghana ragas

Raga: **Naata**
Description:
The Naatta raga invokes a feeling of devotion. It is commonly associated with devotional songs dedicated to Lord Ganesha, making it a preferred choice for opening with, in concerts (kutcheri). It is an enchanting (manoharam) raga. It is derived from a parent scale called Chalanaatta. Naata is one of the ragas classified as "ghana," along with the ragas Gowla, Aarabhi, Varali, and Sree. In the past, the ghana ragas were primarily performed on the veena, a stringed instrument.

Some of the compositions and recommendations in Raga Naatta:
- "Jagadanandakaraka" by Dr. M. Balamuralikrishna
- "Maha Ganapathim" by Yesudas
- "Swaminatha" by Mandolin Srinivas
- "Re Re Manasa Bajare" – Nattai Rupakam

Raga: **Gowla**
Description:
The Gowla raga is one of the Ghana ragas. One of the notes – Rishabham (Ri), sounds very soft and creates a beautiful musical experience. Tyagaraja Swamy's "Dudukugala" and Dikshitar's song "Sri mahaganapathi ravathumam" are wonderful compositions in this raga.
Some of the compositions and recommendations:
- "Dudukugala" rendition by Dr. M. Balamuralikrishna
- "Maha Ganapathim" performed by Yesudas

Raga: **Aarabhi**
Description:
The raga Aarabhi is one of the ghana ragas. One of Tyagaraja Swamy's five gems – Pancha Ratna kriti, "Sadhinchane" is set in this raga. This kriti is like a pendant to the necklace of Pancha Ratna Kritis. It is derived from the parent scale (melakarta) – Dheera Shankarabharanam.

Some of the compositions and recommendations:
- "Sadhinchane" by Dr. M. Balamuralikrishna
- "Nadasudha rasambilanu," the Tyagaraja's composition, discussed above.
- "Sri sarasvati Namostute" sung by M. S. Gopalakrishnan

The ragas Aarabhi and Devagandhari are twins. Devagandhari has veera rasa. It's a real blessing to listen to this raga. "Koluvaiunnade," a kriti in Devagandhari raga, portrays the enchanting aura of Rama as he graces the royal court.

To experience the Devagandhari raga, I recommend listening to
- "Nagaswaram Yalpanam" by P. S. Balamurugan
- "Ksheera sagara sayana"

Raga: **Varali**

Description:

Varali, literally translating to "bumble bee," captures the essence of its gamaka, resembling the buzzing sound of a bee, in this raga. The raga evokes the emotion of karuna rasa (compassion). There are differing opinions regarding its origin. Some suggest that it is derived from the parent scale (melakarta) called Subhapantuvarali, while others argue that it has its roots in Jhalavarali. One of Tyagaraja's Pancha Ratna kritis, "Kanakana Ruchira," was composed in this raga.

Some of the compositions and recommendations include:

- "Kanakana Ruchira" performed by Dr. M. Balamuralikrishna
- "Ka Va Va" by Ranjani – Gayatri, in "A Skanda Sashti Offering"
- "Marakata Mani Varna" by D. K. Pattammal
- "3 Ragam Varali (S Balachander AIR Concert Late 1970s)" – S Balachander's veena performance

Raga: **Sree**
Description:
Sree means "auspicious." The raga is auspicious. It evokes the emotion of karuna rasa (compassion). The timeless composition, "Endaro mahanubhavulu" in Sree ragam by Tyagaraja Swamy, significantly elevated the prominence of this raga.
Some of the compositions and recommendations:
- "Endaro mahanubhavulu"
- "Sri Kamalambike" composed by Muthuswami Dikshitar

Dwitiya ghana ragas are secondary ghana ragas. They are Reetigoula, Narayana goula, Bhouli, Kedaram, and Saranganaata.

Major ragas:

We hear at least one of the famous ragas mentioned below in most concerts. These ragas are significant because they provide a vast musical canvas to artists and the Rasika. Musicians can showcase their creativity by elaborating on the raga, adding "Neraval" (substituting the gist of the raga in the Sahitya phrases while performing tala as per the composition) and "Swara Kalpana," performing these ragas for extended periods, sometimes spanning hours, enthralling the audience. A concert feels complete when one of these ragas is performed.

Composers like Tyagaraja, Muthuswamy Dikshitar, and Syama Sastri created beautiful compositions in these ragas. Technically, these ragas evolved through a process called "Grahabhedam," in which the starting note of a raga is shifted to create a new raga.

Raga: **Todi**

Description:

Todi is considered the king of ragas. In the Telugu language, it means "pull." When someone sings Todi and pulls it off well, it feels like drawing unlimited water from the ocean. It is one of the major, prominent ragas in Carnatic music. The raga has a somber and serious tone, often expressing deep emotions such as yearning and longing. Tyagaraja Swamy composed many kritis (approximately 34 kritis) in this raga.

In Carnatic music concerts, Todi is often performed as a main raga, allowing the artist to explore its vast melodic possibilities through improvisation. The raga can be used in raga therapy to reduce aggressiveness and agitation (medical illness) due to the nature of its notes. There was a renowned Carnatic vocalist, Sitaramayya Garu, who was highly skilled in singing Todi ragam. He was often referred to as "Todi Sitaramayya" due to his expertise in rendering this raga. He was known for performing Todi ragam continuously for eight days, showcasing his deep connection and mastery over this particular raga. There are several compositions such as

- "Kaddanuvariki"
- "Dachukovalena"
- Todi varnam "Eranapai"
- "Dasaradhi nee runamu"

Raga: **Kalyani**

Description:

Kalyani is one of the major, popular ragas in Carnatic music. Its melodic beauty characterizes Kalyani and is often associated with joy and happiness. It's ever-fresh and a refreshing raga for listeners and musicians. The raga evokes bhakti, karuna. It is derived from the parent scale (melakarta) called Mechakalyani. It is a beautiful raga. It is also known as Yaman in Hindustani classical music. Many compositions, including varnams, kritis, and ragamalikas have been composed in Kalyani by various composers over the centuries. The raga can be used in raga therapy to reduce depression (medical illness) due to the nature of its notes. The raga creates hope and a positive atmosphere.

- "Nidhichaala Sukhama" sung by M.S. Subbulakshmi
- "M. S. Gopalakrishnan – RTP Kalyani Ragam"
- "Etavunara kalyani-Tyagaraja-adi- by Ranjani - Gayatri"
- "Mysore V Doraiswamy Iyengar-Ragam Tanam Pallavi-Kalyani-Veenai"

Raga: **Kambhoji**
The mood of the raga: Bhakti (divine)
Description:
Kambhoji raga is also known as "Thakkesi pann" in ancient Tamil music, which dates back to around 3 BCE. This is the oldest known reference to this musical mode. It is a raga derived from the parent scale (melakarta) called Hari Kambhoji. It is said that the raga kambhoji is derived from a country, Cambodia. It is one of the major ragas in Carnatic music. It is widely used in harikatha, yaksha gaanam, slokas, dramas. It evokes a sense of longing and yearning for the divine.
Some of the compositions and recommendations:
- "Kambhoji Ragam – Varnam | Dr L. Subramaniam"
- "O Rangasayee" sung by T. M. Krishna, composed by Tyagararaja Swamy
- "Maa jaanaki chettabattaga" performed by MS Gopalakrishnan
- A tutorial by Ranjani Gayatri with students "Maa Janaki- Kambhoji| RaGa Candid – Shiksha"
- "Evarimaata vinnavo" by Tyagararaja Swamy, sung by M. S. Subbulakshmi
- "Evarimata" by Dr Mani Krishnaswami, for advanced listeners
- "Kailasa nathena" by Dikshitar in chapu talam
- Search for the tag "Raga Khamboji | Malladi Brothers | Carnatic Vocal"

Raga: **Bhairavi**

Description:

Bhairavi is one of the major, prominent ragas in Carnatic music. Bhairav means Lord Shiva. Bhairavi is the goddess Parvati. Kalyani is also the goddess's name.

- "Chintayama" by Shri D. K. Jayaraman
- M. S. Subbulakshmi's "Enati Nomu Phalamo", Bhairavi- Adi- Tyagaraja
- "Bhairavi Raagam – Bhairavi Pravaham" Violin Live Concert by Lalgudi G. Jayaraman – Vol 2"
- "Yaro Ivar Yaro Bhairavi" by D. K. Pattammal

Raga: **Sankarabharanam**

Description:

Sankarabharanam is one of the significant ragas in Carnatic music. This majestic raga, is derived from its parent raga, Dheera Sankarabharanam melakartha. A highly skilled musician named Narasayya, who had great mastery and affection for this raga, was referred to as "Sankarabharanam Narasayya." This raga evokes a serene atmosphere, aiding in inducing sleep for the listeners.

A serpent king rests on Lord Shiva's throat and produces beautiful sounds. The serpent is known as sankarabharanam because the snake listens to the constant music emanating from lord Shiva. The raga can be used in raga therapy to reduce aggressiveness and agitation (medical illness) due to the nature of its notes.

This raga is also called Bilaval in Hindustani music. Here are some recommendations for listening.

- "Swara Raga Sudha" by M. S. Subbulakshmi
- "Swara raga sudha" by N. Ramani (flute)

Raga: **KharaharaPriya**

Om is the first word of Brihat sama in Samaveda, an Indian ancient Veda. The one who renders Samaveda is called the Udgatha. Initially, Samaveda was rendered with three notes, but over time, it evolved to include four, five, six, and eventually seven notes, becoming Sama Gana Murchana and leading to the creation of the Chittaranjani raga. The Kharaharapriya raga was later developed from the Chittaranjani raga.

In the enchanting Chittaranjani raga, there is a popular composition by Tyagaraja Swamy titled "Naada Tanu manisam Sankaram; Namami me manasa sirasa." This kriti expresses reverence to Lord Shiva, acknowledging his body as the Naada, the divine cosmic sound.

Popular compositions include:

- "Pakkala nilabadi" sung by M. S. Subbulakshmi in Chapu talam
- M. S. Subbulakshmi's "Chakkani Raja Margamu"
- "Rama Nee Samanamevaru" by T. M. Krishna

"Naya" ragas, classified as rakti ragas, possess a captivating appeal that makes them highly pleasing to the ears.

There are other ragas that are an integral part of Carrnatic music offering a rich and diverse listening experience.

Raga : **Hamsadhwani**

Description:

The raga evokes bhakti rasa. It is derived from the parent scale (melakarta) called dheera sankarabharanam.

Hamsadhwani means the sound of a swan. Swan (hamsa) is a spiritual symbol in India known for its purest form of wisdom. Paramahamsa is the title of honor applied to spiritual gurus who have become enlightened. In ancient Greece, the swan was regarded as a symbol of beauty and grace. It held a special significance and was considered sacred to the goddess Aphrodite, representing her divine qualities. In Greek mythology, the swan was also revered by Apollo, the god associated with music and various other domains. The swan serves as the divine vehicle for Goddess Saraswati and is renowned for its ability to discern between water and milk. This capacity to discriminate between substances represents its association with wisdom, education, and the ability to differentiate between what is good and what is not. The swan is considered a symbol of intelligence and enlightenment, embodying the qualities of discernment and knowledge.

Hamsadhwani is an excellent choice to begin any concert. It is a perfect opener.

Hamsadhwani is known by the same name in both Hindustani and Carnatic music traditions.
Hamsadhwani raga was introduced to Carnatic and Hindustani music systems by Muthuswamy Dikshitar.
Hamsadhwani is often recommended to be sung in the morning due to its uplifting and refreshing nature.

"Vinayaka ninu" by Veena Kuppayyar

"Vathapi Ganapathim by M. S Subbulakshmi"

M. S. Gopalakrishnan performance of Raag Hamsadhwani – Violin

Some of the compositions & recommendations:

- The composition "Vatapi Ganapatim bhajeham" (means salutations to Lord Ganesha of Vatapi) was set to Hamsadhwani raga.
- "Jalajakshi" – Taanavarnam by Manambuchavidi Venkatasubbayyar

Raga: **Athana**

The mood of the raga: Veera rasa (heroism)

Description: The raga Athana has a unique melodic structure and is known for its devotional flavor. The raga is used in rendering slokas and puranapathanam. It has the ability to create a tranquil atmosphere during performances. "Rara devadi deva" and "Ela ni dayaradu" phrases in "Bala kanaka maya chela" composition show the character and beauty of the raga.

Athana ragam finds its melodic expression in bhajans and purana pathanam, reflecting rama bhakti, affirmation of firm faith, and steadfastly adhering to the path of saranagathi.

Some of the compositions and recommendations:

- "Bala kanakamaya chela" by Tyagararaja Swamy in Aditalam
- "Eela Ni Dayaraadu" renditions of M. S. Subbulakshmi, M. Balamuralikrishna, Nedunuri Krishnamurthy
- "Anupama gunambhudhi" by Tyagararaja Swamy in Adi talam, a wonderful violin performance by A. Kanyakumari, Embar S. Kannan
- "Sri maha ganapathim bhaje", a composition of Dikshitar in Adi talam by Maharajapuram Santhanam

Raga: **Bahudari**

Description:

To my ears, "Bahudari" resonates as "many paths." The notes in this raga convey a sense of versatility as if they have numerous avenues for expression. The raga Bahudaari was created by the revered composer Tyagaraja Swamy. It is derived from the parent scale (melakarta) known as Hari Kambhoji. The raga is an absolute delight for the listeners.

Some of the compositions and recommendations:

- "Brovabharama" by Tyagararaja Swamy, Aditalam sung by T. M. Krishna
- "Brovabarama" by Dr L. Subramaniam
- "Brovabharama" by the Malladi Brothers

Raga: **Sree Ranjani**

Description:

The raga Sree Ranjani is derived from the parent scale (melakarta) known as Kharaharapriya. This rakti raga can be sung at any time.

Tyagaraja Swamy's composition "Sogasuga mridanga talamu" in this kriti is popular.

There is no exact equivalent for the word "sagasu" in English. It encompasses a sense of tender charm and beauty often described in English dictionaries as grace, elegance, and so on. However, the word's true meaning still needs to be discovered in English. This particular composition beautifully embodies the unique charm and beauty of Indian music, the richness of the Telugu language, the essence of devotional tradition, and Tyagaraja's profound love for Rama.

Some of the compositions and recommendations:

- M. S. SubbuLakshmi's "Sogasuga Mridanga Taalamu"
- "Brochevare Vare" – Lalgudi Jayaraman's violin performance
- T. M. Krishna's "Marubalka"
- "Brocevarevare Raghupate" by Nedunuri Krishnamurthy

Raga: **Nalinakanthi**
Description:
The raga was created by the composer Tyagaraja Swamy. The raga mesmerizes the listeners.
Some of the compositions and recommendations:
- "Manaviyalakincha raadate" by Tyagararaja Swamy in Aditalam by M. S. Gopalakrishnan.
- You can also listen to "Manaviyalakincha raadate" performed by Indian rock bands, skillfully remixed with Western instruments, for a delightful musical experience.

Raga: **Saveri**
Description:
The raga evokes karuna rasa. It is derived from the parent scale (melakarta) called Mayamalavagoula. It is a very popular raga. It has a close resemblance to Malahari raga. In the olden days, Malahari raga used to be very popular. Saveri replaced the Malahari raga over some time and became a prominent raga sung or played by many vidwans.
Some of the compositions and recommendations:
- "Sankari Sankuru," a composition by Syama Sastri
- "Rama bana" by Tyagaraja

Raga: **Mukhari**
Description:
The raga evokes the emotion of karuna rasa (compassion). It is derived from the parent scale (melakarta) called NataBhairavi. It is an ancient raga. Mukha + ari in Sanskrit means mukha = face, ari= enemy. Interestingly, the Sanskrit terms "mukha" and "ari" combined suggest an unpleasant or ugly appearance. Therefore, when performing this raga, it is advised to follow it with renditions of Kalyani, Sree Ragam, or Surati to remove any dosha.
Some of the compositions and recommendations:
- "TM Krishna: Ragam Mukhari"
- "Brahmakadigina paadamu" by Annamacharya sung by M. S. Subbulakshmi
- "Entani Ne," a Tyagaraja kriti, by K. V.Narayanaswamy in Rupaka talam

Raga: **Asaaveri**
Description:
The raga evokes bhakti, karuna. It is so captivating that even the serpents find it appealing.
Some of the compositions and recommendations:
- "Rara mayintidaka" by Dr. M. Balamurali Krishna
- DK Pattammal's "Thamasinchuka" varnam, a Patnam Subramanya Iyer composition

Raga: **Amrita Varshini**

Description:

Amrita Varshini means the downpour of nectar. It is derived from the parent scale (melakarta) called Mechakalyani. It is a beautiful raga often known as "the raga of rain." Amritavarshini is the raga that is said to bring showers of rain. Subbarama Dikshitar, in his essential work called Sangita Sampradaya Pradarshini, provides a crucial piece of information about the composition by his grand-uncle Muthuswami Dikshitar. He states that Muthuswami Dikshitar composed a keertana in Amritavarshini raga while he was in Ettayapuram. The composition was inspired by his compassion for the people there who were suffering from a severe drought that had led to the complete destruction of their crops. Legend has it that it had started to rain when Muthuswami Dikshitar was teaching this song to his disciple Subramaniya Ayyar.

Some of the compositions and recommendations:

- "Aanandamrithakarshini" by Veena S. Balachander
- "Alapanai in Amritavarshini" by Dr. Balamuralikrishna
- "M. S. Subbulakshmi's "Anandamruthakarshini"

Raga: **Amrita Vaahini**

Description:

Amrita vaahini means the flow of nectar (amrita pravaham). It is a beautiful raga. The Saramati, Amrita Vaahini, Naaga Gandhari, and Marga Hindolam ragas are catchy ragas, even though they have a limited scope.

Some of the compositions and recommendations:

- "Shri Rama Padama Ni Kripa" in Adi tala, composed by Tyagaraja sung by D. K. Pattamal. One can experience the musical nectar in D. K. Pattammal's voice!
- "Shri Rama Padama" by Dr. K. J. Yesudas
- "Shri Rama Padama" by Saint Tyagaraja, sung by M Balamuralikrishna

Raga: **Anandabhairavi**

Description:

The raga was called "Andhri" in earlier days, which means it's a treasure of Andhra (Telugu people). It is a very popular raga. It evokes bhakti, sringara rasa. It is widely used in dramas, movies, dance performances as well. Many legendary composers have composed this raga, including Tyagaraja, Muthuswami Dikshitar, and Syama Sastri. The beauty of Anandabhairavi gives happiness to the listeners. Apart from the compositions "Ksheera Sagara Vihara" and "Neeke Teliyaka Pote Rama," no other compositions of Tyagaraja Swamy have been found. Some of the compositions:

- Ksheera sagara vihara – Tyagaraja
- Neeke teriyakipote – Tyagaraja
- Marivere – Syama Sastri
- Himachala Tanaya – Syama Sastri
- Manasa guruguha – Dikshitar

Raga: **KannadaGowla**
Description:
The raga evokes bhakti, karuna. It is a very attractive raga. I'd recommend listening to Lalgudi Jayaraman's "Ora Jupu" in Kannadagowla, composed by Tyagaraja. The violin articulates each syllable of the composer's lyrics precisely. In addition, the musical brilliance of Lalgudi Sir is evident as his violin converses with Lord Rama every time the lyrical line repeats, "Oh, Ragoththamaa!". With each repetition, this phrase carries a range of emotions, from a simple statement to a heartfelt sorrow and to inquisitiveness.

Composition and recommendations:
- T. M. Krishna: Raga Kannada Gowla
- Nedunuri Krishnamurthy's rendition of "Sogasu Juda Tarama" in Adi talam, by Tyagaraja
- Mandolin Shrinivas' performance of "Sogasu Chuda Tharama" from Soorya Festival

Raga: Kanada
Description:
The raga evokes bhakti, karuna. It is derived from the parent scale (melakarta) called Kharaharapriya.

Some of the compositions and recommendations:
- Dr. L. Subramaniam – Raga Kanada
- "Alaipayuthe kanna" sung by Sudha Raghunathan

Raga: **Khamas**

Description:

Khamas is an attractive raga. It is inspired by North Indian music. It evokes sringara rasa. It holds an ancient lineage. In the Tamil music system, this raga is referred to as Pancha Chamaram. The Khamas raga is beautiful and listeners always enjoy listening to it. Some of the compositions and recommendations:

- "Maate Malayadhwaja" – Daru Varnam by M. S. Subbulakshmi
- "Sujanajeevana" | Akashvani Sangeet by D. K. Pattammal

Raga: **Chakravakam**

Description:

Chakravakam is a very vibrant raga. The raga evokes bhakti, karuna. It is also a music scale by itself. It is also called Ahir bhairav raga in Hindustani style of music. We can sing this raga at all times. It was called "Toya vegavaahini" in Venkatamakhi times. When we do graha bhedam for the madhyamam swara, it gives Sarasangi raga.

Some of the compositions and recommendations:

- P Unnikrishnan – Gajananayutam Ganeshvaram
- "Sugunamule Cheppukonti" by Sri. Vijay Siva in Lasya – The Culture Hub
- "1974 – Akashvani Sangeet Sammelan" by Lalgudi J. Jayaraman's Violin Recital

Raga: **Dhanyasi**

Description:

The raga evokes bhakti, karuna. It is derived from the parent scale (melakarta) called Hanumattodi. The listener feels satisfied saying "dhanyosmi" while listening to the raga.

Some of the compositions and recommendations:

- "Sangita jnanamu bhaktivina"

Raga: **Natakuranji**
Description:
It is a beautiful raga. An Apoorva raga. It is full of bhava expressions, and creates a musical atmosphere. Some of the compositions and recommendations:
- "Chalamela" tana varnam
- "Srinivasa varadayaka" by Dr. Nookala Chinna Satyanarayana

Raga: **Mayamalavagowla**
Description:
The raga evokes bhakti, karuna, shanta rasa. Purandara dasar introduced the raga for beginners to learn carnatic music. It can create a very soothing effect. Some of the compositions & recommendations:
- "Tulasidala" by MS Subbulakshmi, a Tyagaraja swami kriti
- "Srinathadi" by DK Pattammal, a Dikshitar kriti

Raga: **Bilahari**
Description:
The raga evokes bhakti, sringara rasa. The mention of Tyagaraja Swamy singing the song "Na Jeevadhara" suggests a powerful narrative where it is believed that the saint's music had the ability to bring a deceased person back to life. This story reflects the profound impact of the raga, and spiritual significance attributed to Tyagaraja Swamy's compositions.
Some of the compositions and recommendations:
- "Dorakuna" sung by S. Ramanathan

Raga: **Brindavanasaranga**
Description:
It is an attractive raga, an Apoorva raga.
Some recommendations include:
- "Rangapura vihara" sung by various artists and music bands like M. S Subbulakshmi, T. M. Krishna.
- Another popular composition by Tyagaraja Swamy is "Kamalaptakula."

Raga: **Mohana**

Description:

It is a raga used for deep meditation. Sammohana "mohana," a very attractive raga, is attributed to Lord Krishna's mesmerizing flute. Listeners can feel the positive essence of the raga. There are so many songs in the raga. It has veera rasam.

Some of the compositions :

- "Mohana rama"
- "Nagalingam namami"

Raga: **Reethigowla**

Description:

The raga evokes bhakti. Reetigowla and Anandabhairavi ragas are like twins.

Some of the compositions and recommendations:

- "Janani ninuvina" sung by M. S. Subbulakshmi

Raga: **Vasantha**

Description:

The raga of spring season. It has a very delightful presence, being the raga of bhakti rasam and expression. My guru D. K. Pattamal taught me "Marakatha lingam chintaye" kriti in this raga.

Some of the compositions and recommendations:

- "Sitamma mayamma" sung by M. S. Subbulakshmi
- "Ramachandram"

Raga: **Hindola**
Description:
The raga evokes bhakti, karuna. The most popular raga. It's a very attractive raga in the pentatonic (five notes) scales. In the past, some performers would sing Hindolam raga with the musical note Chatusruti Dhaivatam.

Some of the compositions and recommendations:
- "Samarjavaragamana – Hindola M. S. Gopalakrishnan"
- "Manasuloni" by Srirangam Gopalaratnam"

Raga: **Sahana**

Description:

The raga evokes a sense of devotion and tranquility (bhakti, shanta rasa). It is derived from the parent scale (melakarta) called Hanumattodi. Compositions like "Ee Vasudha," "Ee Manatichevu", "Giripai Nelakonna," and "Emanatichevu" by Tyagaraja Swamy are popular. When a musician sings this raga, it instantly creates a musical atmosphere. Pure Carnatic music style ragam which has very unique expressions.

Some of the compositions and recommendations:

- "Sahana – eevasudha"
- "Sahana – vandanamu"
- "K. V. Narayanaswamy – Ragam Tanam Pallavi – Sahana"

Raga: **Shanmukhapriya**

Description:

The raga is also called "Chamaram." Chamaram means a breeze from a fan and the raga is associated with Lord Subramanya, also known as Shanmukha, with six faces.

Some of the compositions and recommendations:

- "Marivere – shanmukhapriya" composed by Patnam Subramanya Iyer.
- Ragam Tanam Pallavi in Shanmukhapriya Raga

Raga: **Surati**

Description:

The raga is sung at the end of the concert. If the beginning of the concert raga is for Naatta, then Surati is at the end of the concert. Surati also means a breeze from hand fan.

Some of the compositions and recommendations:

- "Geetharthamu"

Raga: **Begada**:

Description:

The raga is the favorite raga of most of the musicians. It's a very attractive raga. It is an auspicious raga. Bedaga is like "meegada" – butter with cream from milk. Great vidwans such as Voleti Venkateswara explored more on this raga.

Some of the compositions and recommendations:

- "Sankari nee begada" sung by Voleti Venkateswarlu
- "K. V. Narayanaswamy – Ragam Tanam Pallavi – Begada"

Desya ragas: These ragas are foreign ragas to south Indian music. I have mentioned some of the ragas below.

> Raga: **Sindhubhairavi**
> Description:
> This raga is a very catchy raga. "Sindhu" refers to Sindhu/ Indus which is one of the longest rivers in the world. "Visweswar darishan kar" "Rama rama yanarada" compositions are very popular.

Raga: **Kaapi**

Description:

The raga evokes karuna rasa. It is usually sung at the end of the music concert or after the concert's first half. It is lovely listening to this raga.

Kaapi is a versatile raga that can evoke various emotions, such as devotion, and introspection. In Tyagaraja's composition "Neevalla gunadoshamemi" Tyagaraja introspects himself. "Intasoukya" composition in this raga by Tyagaraja Swamy explains the greatness and beauty of music.

Some of the compositions and recommendations include:

- "M. S. Subbulakshmi- Jagadodharana- Kapi- Purandharadasa-Adi"
- "Inta Saukyamani-Kapi-adi-Tyagaraja- Taniavartanam- Dwaram Ventkataswamy Naidu- Violin"
- "T. M. Krishna w/ Sheik Mahaboob Subhani and Smt. Kaleeshabi Mahaboob: Jagadodharana"
- "Intasowkhya-Bombay Jayashri- Raga Kapi"
- "Kapi at Ragasudha Hall"

> Raga: **Yamuna Kalyani**
> Description:
> "Yamuna" refers to the Yamuna river which is the river that witnessed the love of Lord Krishna and Gopis. Kalyani raga in Carnatic Music is equivalent to Yaman in Hindustani style of Music. This raga is about the Kalyani raga (Yaman) at the Yamuna river, known as Yamuna Kalyani. K. J. Yesudas's rendition of "Krishnane Begane Baro" is incredibly soothing and delightful to the ears. "Haridasulu Vedale" by Tyagaraja Swamy is another exceptional composition, showcasing his genius in music.
> D. K. Jayaraman's "Jambupate" is a wonderful rendition of Dikshitar's
> Penchabhuta linga kriti on Water.

There are other beautiful ragas like Behag, Dwijanvanthi, Desh, etc., that we must listen to, to receive aesthetic bliss.

Numerous ragas captivate the listeners, and among beginners' favorites are the pentatonic ragas with five notes, including Mohana, Madhyamavathi, Suddha Dhanyasi, Suddha Saveri, Hamsadhwani, and Hindola. Other ragas like Sourashtra, Hamsanandi, Devagandhari, Neelambari are very popular. I search for the raga and listen to the various renditions of wonderful artists.

Tyagaraja Swamy's songs are deep and make us think about both the lyrics and the music. The poetic expression suggests that Rama's Kodhanda (bow) showers numerous ragas, inspiring musicians to create blissful melodies from these divine musical elements.

In the song "Sarasa sangathi sandarbhamu giramulura." The words spoken by Rama are like neraval and sangatis in Carnatic music, which adds to the beautification and improvisation of musical expressions of a raga. These patterns add layers of meaning and depth to the melody, much like the way in which Rama's words carried significance in ancient tales. It's like the musical language of the bow and arrows, telling a story through their harmonious expressions.

Tyagaraja Swamy's "Samajavaragamana" in Hindola raga beautifully portrays Lord Rama's walk as musical, illuminating the saptaswara -- the seven notes which came from Veda.

It is said "Anantavai Ragaha," signifying the infinite nature of ragas.

O Lord of infinite ragas, I offer my salutations to you! You are cosmic, and your creations are uniquely splendid. Your melodious presence is felt everywhere as the gamakas of the ragas. Countless devotees sing your praises, including the most eminent devotees like

Tyagaraja, Dikshitar, Syama Sastri, Purandaradasa, Kanakadasa, Ramadasu, Narayana Theertha, Sadasiva Brahmendra, Meera, Kabirdas, Arunachala kavi, Jayadeva, Arunagirinathar, and Andal.

Muthuswamy Dikshitar

Syama Sastri

Saint Thyagaraja Swamy

Vijaya Vittala Temple, Hampi, UNESCO Heritage Site India

References

Venkata Rama Iyer, T. L. Muthuswamy Dikshitar. National Book Trust, 1968.

Sumathi Krishanan, Muthuswami Deeshitar and Tiruvarur, 2005.

NaTarAja – symbolism. Aavilable from: sanskritdocuments.org

Kamisetti Srinivasulu (original), translated by K. Selva. "Annamacharya." TTD publication.

University of Central Florida, "Your Brain on music". Pegasus magazine.

Vidya Chivukula, Shivaraman Ramaswamy. Effect of Different Types of Music on Rosa Chinensis Plants. International Journal of Environmental Science and Development. 2014; 5(5)..

Dr. Nookala Chinna Satyanarayana. "Raga Lakshana Sangraham".

Srabani Maharara, Dr. Niranjan Sabar. The concept of 'OM': (with special reference to chāndogya upanisad).

International Journal of Sanskrit Research. 2020; 6(3): 04–09

Niraaghaatam Sri Ramakrishna Sastry. "Sri Muthuswami Deekshita Kriti Manideepika".

Amirthalingam Murugesan. "SACRED TANKS OF SOUTH INDIA", published by researchgate.net

P. Sambamoorthy. "Great Musicians", published by The Indian music Publishing House.

Dr. Nookala Chinna Satyanarayana. A monograph on Sri Tyagaraja Swamy's Ghana raga pancharatna keertanas.

Glossary

Ajapa natanam: A unique dance performed in South India, specifically associated with the deity Lord Shiva at the Ajapa Mandapam.

Ananda Tandava: The dance of bliss performed by Lord Shiva as Nataraja, the cosmic dancer.

Bhajans: Devotional songs sung in India.

Bhakti: Devotional love or devotion, a central theme in many Indian music compositions.

Carnatic music: A system of Indian classical music originating in South India.

Dasara: A ten-day Hindu festival that celebrates the victory of good over evil.

Dhrupad: A form of Indian classical vocal music, known for its seriousness and emphasis on slow tempos and improvisation.

Gamaka: Ornaments or embellishments used in Indian classical music.

Ghatam: A South Indian clay pot percussion instrument used in various music traditions, including Carnatic music.

Guru: A teacher or mentor in Indian classical music tradition.

Harikatha: A storytelling art form accompanied by Carnatic music.

Hindustani music: A system of Indian classical music originating in North India.

Jala lingam: The water linga, one of the five sacred Shiva lingas representing the five elements.

Jugalbandi: A musical performance featuring a duet between two lead instrumentalists.

Kriti: A composed song in Carnatic music, often with devotional themes.

Mela: A parent scale in Carnatic music, similar to a mode in Western music.

Mridangam: A South Indian percussion instrument, often played alongside the violin in Carnatic music concerts.

Muktai Swaram: Open notes played individually in a composition.

Mudra: A signature or mark used by a composer to identify themselves within their compositions.

Muthuswami Dikshitar: A renowned composer of Carnatic music in the 18th–19th century.

Nada Yoga: The practice of using sound as a path to spiritual realization.

Nataraja: The dancing aspect of Lord Shiva, also known as the cosmic dancer.

Om (Aum): A sacred syllable in Hinduism, considered to be the primordial sound and embodiment of Brahman.

Pancha Bhuta Linga Kshetras: Five sacred sites in South India associated with Lord Shiva, each representing one of the five elements.

Pancha Nadai: The five elements (earth, water, fire, air, and space) are believed to be represented by the five syllables used in solfege in Carnatic music.

Prana: The life force energy in yogic tradition.

Raga Alapana or Alap: An improvised exploration of a raga, showcasing its nuances and emotions.

Sabha: A venue dedicated to the performance of Indian classical music.

Samaveda: One of the four Vedas, focusing on melodies and chants.

Sanskrit: An ancient Indo-Aryan language, the primary language of Hinduism, and a classical language of India.

Saptaswara: The seven musical notes in Indian classical music.

Sargam: The solfege system used in Indian classical music, consisting of the seven notes: Sa, Ri (or Re), Ga, Ma, Pa, Dha, and Ni.

Shishya parampara: The disciple tradition in Indian classical music, where knowledge and skills are passed down from teachers to students.

Shruti: A microtone in Indian music, smaller than a semitone.

Sitar: A string instrument plucked with a sliding plectrum, used in Hindustani music.

Swaram (Svara): A musical note in Indian music.

Tala: The rhythmic structure of a composition, defined by a specific meter and time signature.

Telugu: A Dravidian language spoken in the Indian states of Andhra Pradesh and Telangana.

Temple: A place of worship associated with a particular religion.

Thalam: Another term for Tala, referring to the rhythmic cycle.

Veena: A string instrument from India, played by plucking the strings with a plectrum.

Veda: A collection of four ancient religious texts in Hinduism, considered to be the oldest scriptures of the world.

Vijaya Vittala Temple: A UNESCO World Heritage Site temple in Hampi, India, famous for its musical pillars.

Violin: A string instrument, though not originally from India, that has become a prominent accompanying instrument in South Indian music concerts and can also be featured in solo performances.

Acknowledgments

I offer my heartfelt respects to my guruji, Nadanidhi, Padmabhushan, Dr. Nookala Chinna Satyanarayana, whose guidance introduced me to the world of raga music. He taught me the depths of music, be it theory or learning compositions. He is a constant source of inspiration to me. This book is a token of my love and gratitude to my guru on the occasion of his birth centenary.

I offer my salutations to my music gurus Smt. Ammaji, "Veena Vidwan" Sri Sista Suryanarayana, Sangeetha Kalanidhi D.K. Pattammal, Dr. Sabari Girish. I am grateful to my music teacher, Dr. Sabari Girish, head of the Department of Vocal Music at SV College of Music and Dance, who read this book and provided valuable suggestions, and guidance.

I extend my salutations to my parents, who encouraged me to follow music as my passion.

I owe my sincere thanks to Smt. Dr Challa Prabhavathi, Retired Principal of SV College of Music and Dance; Sri Nookala Annaji Rao; Sri S. Dakshina Murthy Sarma, Dean, National Sanskrit University, Tirupati; Sri Shivaram Vinjamuri; Sangeetacharya Sri Dr Vyzarsu Balasubrahmanyam; Smt. Sarada Kasivajhala,

Founder, Valley Veika Channel, USA; Smt Dr. Dwaram Lakshmi,grand-daughter of legendary violin maestro Dwaram Venkataswami Naidu; Smt Dr. Sudha Kalavagunta, Kuchipudi Dancer, USA; Billy Lease, music educator, Guitar teacher, USA; Sri Bhaskar Ganti, CEO, International Software Systems Inc, USA; Prof. N. Padma, Sri Dr. Manda Ananta Krishna, Sri Dr. Chakalakonda Ramakantha Rao; Sri K.V.R.Subrahmanyam, Smt Kasivajjula Suryakumari; Sri Naveen Kolli; Sri Rambhotla Ramesh; Smt. Cheruvu Lalitha Kameswari; Dr. K.S.Viswanatham for their encouragement.

My heartfelt thanks to Debapriya Adhikary, hindustani vocalist; Srividya Venkat, Indian Carnatic Violinist and Teacher, United Kingdom; Mahesh Cheemalapati, USA; Sriram Ramaswamy, Canada; Maruvada Mani Shankar; Dr. Aasish Pappu, USA; Throvagunta Venkata Sesha Rajeshwar (TVS), Creator of Spiritual CheatSheet Youtube channel for all their help and support.

I wish to thank Sri Bhaskar Rao for his beautiful paintings. I wish to acknowledge Sambavi Vigneswaran's great contribution to the book cover design and illustrations, including her reviews and suggestions.

My heartfelt gratitude to my musical friends Dr. K.Subramanyam; Music Director Sridhar Athreya; Padmaja Sonti; Kalyan Ramachandran; Music Producer S.Jaykumar; Singer and Music Composer Sai Sreekanth; Singer Saandip; Playback singer and Composer Ram Prasad; Nihaal, Matangi School of Arts; Singer Nitya Santoshini, Dr. Potharaju Girija Seshamamba, Founder Chairman of Sree Sesha Sai Sangeeta Academy; Music teacher and Author of Indian Music books Dr. P.Surya Narayana; Migada Venkat, Founder & Chairman at SaamaVeda Music Academy;

Acknowledgments

Singer Smt. Sunitha Balaji;Guitarist Vinod babu; Singer, Composer Smt. Lakshmi Pucchha; Carnatic musicians Vidushi Smt.Subbalakshmi Somayajula, Ramya Ravada, P.Sriramulu, T.P.Chakrapani, Panduranga Sarma, Nallanchakravarthula Parthasarathi, TPBS Balasubramanian,Paravastur Srinivas Gopalan, Bandi Sarma, Raghvendra Prasad, "Naama Sankeertana Dhurina" Brahma Sree Nukala Yagna Satya Narayana Sarma Bhagavatar, Nemani Raja for inspiring me musically.

I thank my friends and relatives for their constant support.

I would like to express my gratitude to my wife, Sailaja Maruvada, and my daughter, Sree Valli Maruvada, for their invaluable help and support in completing this book. Sailaja assisted me with proofreading, while Sree Valli helped me select the paintings, illustrations, and fonts for the book.

Finally, to my readers, thank you for picking up this book. I hope you find something within its pages that resonates with you.

This journey wouldn't have been possible without each and every one of you.

With deepest gratitude,

Bheema Shankar

Praises For The Book

"*H*amsadhwani" is a captivating exploration of music and spirituality. From Ustad Bismillah Khan's mystical meeting with Bhagwan Shri Krishna to Sarabha Sastrigal's mesmerizing flute melodies, each chapter resonates with the transformative power of music to unite souls with the divine. Bheema Sankar's Hamsadhwani is an essential reading for creative musicians and music lovers. With best wishes.

– **Dr Manda Anantha Krishna,**
Flautist, SV College of Music and dance, TTD, Tirupati

Bheema Shankar, pours his heart out and opens the door towards the vast and enchanting universe of Carnatic music in these pages. Whether you are a seasoned musician, an aspiring aficionado, or simply a curious explorer of the arts, this book will serve as a guiding light on your journey through the mesmerizing world of Carnatic music. Its melodies will resonate in your heart, its rhythms will awaken your spirit, and its wisdom will inspire a lifelong pursuit of musical enlightenment.

– **Saandip,**
Playback Singer and actor

Praises For The Book

I'm very happy to say I've known Bheema Shankar for three decades now, and he's not just a good friend but also a Carnatic classical musician and a remarkable music artist. Despite his IT career, he dedicates his time to enriching the music community. Under the tutelage of Dr. Nookala Chinna Satyanarayana, we both honed our musical skills for years. Bheema has gathered his musical insights and crafted a fantastic book that promises to be invaluable for generations to come. Wishing him all the best!

– Sri Pedapenki SriRamulu,
Music Diploma, Sangeetha Praveena,
Author of "SangeethamritaVarshini"

"Hamsadhwani" is an interesting read for music lovers and connoisseurs of music. It helps them develop an authentic understanding of the age-old Indian music tradition. It is a brilliant narrative because all the anecdotes, history of temples, personalities, and song references contained in this book are presented very well for the readers to engage with.

– Bhaskar Ganti,
CEO, International Software Systems Inc, USA

Bheema Shankar unearthed the precious gems from the musical ocean, elucidating the musical intricacies of South Indian music to both musicians and laymen alike. Bheema Shankar has delicately captured the essence of every dimension of Carnatic music with exceptional grace and exquisite beauty.

May divine blessings shower upon him and his family. Sending my best wishes to all readers of the book.

– Lakshmi Venkata Puchha,
Singer and music composer, USA

Praises For The Book

I've heard that Indian classical music is not just entertainment; it is designed to elevate one's consciousness. This book got me closer to experiencing this. A masterpiece by Bheema Shankar that will take you back in time and make you look at Indian classical music with a renewed perspective.

– Sriram Ramaswamy,
Guitar Instructor, Co-founder of Caninsoft Inc, Canada

It is with great admiration for Mr. Shankar's work that I recommend to you is his latest victory, Hamsadhwani. As I immersed myself in Mr.Shankar's exploration of Indian Carnatic music, I found myself transported to a realm where divine melodies intertwined with celestial rhythms. His vivid accounts of Ajapa Mandapam's sacred dance rituals and Muthuswamy deekshitar's Pancha Bhuta Linga Kritis revealed the profound depths of Carnatic music.

Mr.Shankar's insightful narrative unveils the symbolism behind Nataraja's cosmic dance, each movement resonating with the eternal cycles of creation, preservation, and destruction. From the celestial 'OM' radiating around Nataraja to the symbolic significance of his earrings, every detail is meticulously explored, offering a profound glimpse into the timeless wisdom of Indian mythology and spirituality. Through the book, Mr.Shankar invites readers on a transformative journey, where music becomes a conduit for spiritual enlightenment and cultural understanding. I wish Mr. Shankar all the best and I have no doubt in my mind that his book will be a raging success.

– Dr. Sudha Kalavagunta,

Artistic Director of Lasya sudha Dance Academy, M.Comm, M.A Kuchipudi dance, Ph.D in Performing arts (Telugu University) and Ph.D in Performing arts (Dravidian University)

Praises For The Book

The elegantly named book "Hamsadhwani" signifies an auspicious beginning. Hamsadhwani stands as a splendid introductory raga. I hope the book achieves resounding success, and I hope Bheema Shankar continues to grace us with more auspicious creations in the future.

– Sridhar Athreya, Music Director

The unseen facet of art finds its manifestation through uninterrupted practice and creative passion. When a sense of devotion and an ability to connect with nature arise, an artist acquires gifted meditative faculties. As part of his exploration, an evolved artist delves into myriad angles of art.

Mr. Bheema Sankar, an intimate friend, has precisely accomplished this through his valuable book 'Hamsadhwani'. Remarkably, he has not confined himself to the nuances of music in his book; instead, he has incorporated metaphysics, painting, temple architecture, as well as nature's splendor into his work. It is believed that yogic saints attain Mukti through the sound vibrations from swans of the Manasa Sarovara. Hamsadhwani is a raga renowned for leading the performer to enlightenment as it is free from the Madhyama and Daivatha points. Mr. Bheema Sankar, who has authored a book titled Hamsadhwani for the benefit of music students, could well be termed as a Sangeetha Yoga Sadhaka and Suswara Upasaka. I hope that this precious book, which elucidates the valuable basics of Indian Music, will attain its coveted place in world literature. I pray that the work will stand as a torchbearer in its own right.

– Dr. K.Subramanyam, PhD in Music

About The Author

$\mathcal{F}$or the past thirty years, Bheema Shankar has been deeply immersed in the world of music, serving as a music teacher, mentor, singer, lyric writer, and music composer. He received initial training from Smt. Ammaji, Veena Vidwan Sri Sista Suryanarayana Murthy, Padmabhushan Sri Dr. Nookala Chinna Satyanarayana and valuable tutelage from "Sangeetha kalanidhi" Padma Vibhushan D. K. Pattammal. While in Tirupati, he attended TTD colleges and learned music from Dr. A. Sabari Girish.

Bhimashankar's contributions to the music industry are remarkably diverse, spanning roles as a playback singer, music director, and creator of music for various mediums, including films, short films, devotional music albums, Punjabi albums, jingles, and fusion music concerts. His successful collaboration with Subramanyam resulted in the creation of "Tolidaivam," "Bhakti Tarangalu," "Mukti Mandaralu" music albums. One of the standout performances in his career involves singing the "Bhagavad Gita" in Telugu across various ragas, earning repeated telecasts on Doordarshan. Collaborating with the legendary singer S. P. Balasubramanyam and other playback singers showcased his exceptional compositional skills. He works with various artists in India, the Netherlands, and United States on music projects.

Bheema Shankar received blessings from spiritual leaders such as Sri Paramacharya of Kanchi, Chinna Jeeyar Swami, Yerpedu Swamiji, Swami Mukundananda, Pujya Sri Sunkesula Ratnabala His successful collaboration with Sreedhar Athreya resulted in the creation of "Chinnari Chitti Geethalu," a Telugu jingle music album with animation that gained immense popularity with numerous hits on YouTube. Also composed music for Telugu films. He has sung in various places such as Shilpa Kala Vedika, Ravindra Bharati, Telugu University, and SV Auditorium.

In the digital realm, Bheema Shankar actively contributes to platforms like the Humm Bhakti channel, Spiritual, devotional channels on YouTube, and lends his voice to SVBC and other TV channels.

About The Author

His wide-ranging engagement in the field is evident through his participation in All India Radio music programs, TV shows, and interviews.

Bheema Shankar's musical journey further includes rendering the Bhagavad Gita in various ragas and participating in over 25 episodes of the Carnatic music series "Saptaswaralu" on Doordarshan, a national TV channel in India. Beyond his performances, he has composed hundreds of songs, appeared on TV shows, and authored articles on music, which have found a place in esteemed music magazines.

For the past twenty years, he's been an IT professional, catering to Fortune 500 clients, while also creating music for corporate companies. Shankar conducts a number of lecture demonstrations and writes research articles. He hosts complimentary workshops on ragas to promote awareness of Indian classical music.

Let's connect

BheemaShankar.net (OR) https://bheemashankar.net

Email: SHANKAR.MARUVADA@GMAIL.COM

Made in the USA
Monee, IL
03 May 2026

49438748R00142